INVOKED

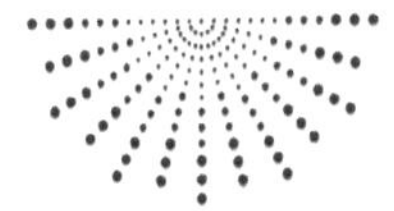

DANI KRISTOFF

Love can conquer many things ...

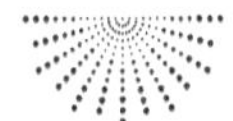

Earl Pressonville sucked in a breath as Pris Denholm glided down the stairs, her crimson robe parting to reveal smooth white skin, rounded breasts and long, sleek legs. His pulse thrummed as he thought of her beauty and the keen edge of danger she represented. A smile lifted the corner of her mouth as her gaze tracked over him. The expression in her eyes, though, was cold and dark, with no glint of sexual attraction, no heat of desire. Earl swallowed. Doubt infiltrated his ego, like the creep of a spider across bare skin. She wanted him, didn't she?

For months now he'd been trying to get her attention, vying to be her consort. As she reached the bottom of the stairs, his breath hitched. Being up close and personal with all that dark, seething magic she exuded, was as tantalizing as it was perilous. He was going to drink in her sexual power. Just thinking about what was going to happen next sent a shudder through him and teased his erection with need. Out of all the warlocks and humans that flocked around her, she'd chosen him, at last.

Her robe slid from her shoulders and glided

gently to the floor, leaving her naked before him. Her body was that of a Titian Venus, pale, bold and full of sexual promise. The eyes, though, brought goose-bumps to his flesh as there was something empty in them, empty and brittle. He became conscious of the straps holding him to the dentist chair and how they cut into the skin of his wrists and ankles. This was not how he'd imagined his moment of triumph. This was not how he would amaze her with his physical prowess.

Earlier, he'd arrived at her house and let himself into the audience room which was usually packed with her followers. It had been empty—just a few stained cushions and a couple of beer bottles that had dribbled pale liquid on the shabby, once-white carpet. He'd wondered if she was going to allow him to see her alone. Was their coupling not to be a spectacle like the ones he'd witnessed? The memory of her rutting with other warlocks had made him so hard he'd thought his cock would burst. His best friends had fucked her and all he had wished while watching them was that it was him. He wanted to lick and suck her moist clit and hear her moan as her ecstasy washed over them all. It was all he thought about, day and night.

He didn't know how he'd come to be down here in a basement tied to a chair. But he wanted to be there.

She turned her back to him and he couldn't see what she was doing. The air thickened, with scent, with need, with tentacles of magic. He shook his head, trying to clear it. A haze of incense teased his nostrils—powdery sandalwood and sweet jasmine. He breathed in deeply. Then time stood still and when he next looked around he realized he'd been out cold. Some unnamed dread lingered in the back of his mind. *Something isn't right!* His gaze travelled over walls the color of dark wine. It was the old house, Pris's place, but his first time below the stairs.

Pris turned, and a frisson of fearful delight sped up his spine. Anticipation widened his eyes, made his breath catch. 'Pris,' he whispered, his tongue feeling thick, his throat parched.

Her eyes didn't react but there was a hint of a smile around her full mouth. 'Earl Pressonville, how good of you to offer yourself to me.'

He struggled to see in the dimness. The flames of tea-light candles flickered and blurred. Her pale skin glowed and drew his attention. He fought the pull of her spell and looked away. Glancing up, he saw two small, blackened windows near the ceiling. An escape route. Like a shout from the darkness, his mind voice urged. *Run! Now!*

Too late! She was there again—filling his vision with her loveliness. He was so hot for her he couldn't look away. He wanted her, wanted to be there. He was hard and ready. So hard, he ached and throbbed and thought he'd die of want. He was desperate, needy. For six months his sheets had been soaked in sweat and cum all from thoughts of her, of how she moved, talked, magicked. This was the moment. He couldn't back out now.

He jerked an arm, but his flesh strained against the restraints. *Trapped!* Panic trilled through his blood. He feared being restrained, yet his eyes could only drink in the sight of her, and her magic soothed his apprehension.

Her gaze appraised him and she sucked on her bottom lip. Then she wound the mechanism of the chair, stretching him out to lie horizontally. Still no hint of warmth from her, no flush of desire. Her look was clinical.

'What are you doing?' he asked hoarsely.

'Keep quiet. You'll interrupt my concentration and I need it for the ritual.'

He lifted his head and gaped at her. Closing his mouth, he laughed the comment off. 'Yeah right, ritual fuck.'

There was a rustle of something and then a sting. 'I said keep quiet.'

He was too surprised to cry out, even though the lash across his stomach smarted. She thwacked him again as he gripped the arm of the chair and growled through the pain.

'Wait. Wait. I didn't sign ...' Too late. The lash came again and something happened inside. It hurt but his erection grew even harder. Words feathered around his ears as she chanted, timing her strokes to the end of each line. Sometimes soft. Sometimes hard. Across his legs, his shoulders, his thighs, the strokes fell, just missing his erect penis, which was a granite spear of pain.

As his yells and cries lifted to the floor above he realized this wasn't anything like the shows he'd seen upstairs. They'd been kinky, on the edge a bit, but this was doing things to his brain.

He moaned until her small hand caressed his balls. His whimpers died as she stroked the sore flesh of his stomach and chest. Anticipation rose inside. What would she do next?

'That was—'

'I didn't tell you to talk. Shut it.'

Trembling and weak, he quietened. Surprisingly, his erection remained. Hadn't he come already? Clearly not, because as the whipping had ceased, he could still feel the pain in his cock. It was going to explode.

She tightened the bindings on his hands and feet

again, then lowered the chair so it was knee-height. This was it. She was finally going to fuck him. His breath hitched and his erection twitched. Elegantly, she straddled him, holding herself above him and catching his eye. Then she lowered herself. She had a landing strip of pubic hair and her inner lips were dark and swollen as they consumed his erection. Slick and hot, she covered him completely, her head thrown back, her abs rippling and her stomach muscles clenching. He tried to hold back the shout of pleasure and then she rose up, ready to ride.

Mesmerized, he watched her. It was the moment. They were shagging, finally. He'd wanted to pleasure her with his mouth. He'd wanted to hear her cries, master her and have her adore him. There'd been none of that. She was calling the shots. He was the thing that was being played. This was not sharing.

At the back of his mind, he wanted out. He wished he'd listened to his instinct and not come down here. It was a marvelous fuck but something wasn't right.

Her movements were hard and fast. She was power and muscle. He watched his cock disappear inside her, the rapid movements enthralling. Why hadn't he come? He wanted to. He wanted to blow and get the hell out of there.

The words of her chant fell around his ears. Glancing up, he saw her eyes ablaze with light. Magic stirred the air around him. Then he caught the glint of a knife, golden and bejeweled. Held above her head, it glowed in the candlelight as she rode him hard. He tried to focus, to pull the strands of his intellect and magic together. The ties on his wrists burned like flame. The ones on his ankles too. By the deities, he was not coming near this woman again.

A burning sensation erupted in his solar plexus.

Aghast, he looked down at the blood welling from the cut. He screamed and came and his power shot out of him, straight into her. Her mouth hovered over the wound, drawing in his magic.

Blood magic! No!

Weakness spread through him, making his limbs turn to lead, then he realized it was more than having his magic stolen. It was him she was stealing. His life force dragged from his helpless body, which was wrapped in befuddlement and restraints. Her skin seemed to swell, and her eyes burned so bright that the flesh surrounding them darkened.

No, not like this. Earl wasn't going to die. He was going to fight. Resisting the last pull of her mouth, he sequestered a bit of himself away. Yet, as his chest stopped moving and his body hung unresponsive in its restraints, he knew that there wasn't much hope. His spirit was alive but he was trapped in his dead body.

The dark witch Pris dismounted his lifeless corpse, a satisfied smile on her face, and then she leaned in to suck the last of the cum from the tip of his cock. He tried to fight back, tried to hold on to that last drop until she stopped. But he was powerless and bodiless.

Maybe it was that unwillingness to give up that helped him cling to some vestige of life. Aware, but bound to a sack of flesh that no longer lived and breathed, he was helpless to fight against his situation.

❦

They'd taken him to the old ruin next door, lifted the floorboards and dug a hole. Two of her human followers had tossed him in and shoveled dirt on top. He realized that there were others there in the ground with him. The friends he'd thought had taken their pleasure in Pris and then pissed off long ago. They were dead, truly dead. Unlike him.

Later, as time rotted the flesh around him, Earl brooded, a dark silent rage that allowed no light. He castigated himself and ranted at the universe.

A whole thirty years passed in the darkness. All hope faded. He was cloaked in despair and pain. But he still wasn't dead.

There was nothing he could do to alter his situation.

CHAPTER ONE

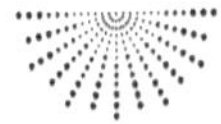

Nea hauled the basket of groceries out of the car and lugged it up the path to Mary Parson's door. As the screen door was unlocked, she opened it, then she continued on in. 'It's only me,' she called to the darkened interior.

'Put them on the bench in the kitchen, dear,' Mary said from her rocker.

'Hello. Sorry I'm late,' Nea said as she walked through to the rear of the house and began unloading. She slipped the milk into the fridge, along with the cat's food. A ball of fur brushed against her bare leg.

'Hello Bart,' she said and bent down to rub her fingers along the cat's spine.

She put the kettle on and prepared some tea. 'So, Mary, how are you feeling today?'

'I'm doing about the same, dear. I'm sorry to be a trouble.' Her feeble voice reached Nea from the front sitting room.

She detected the depression in Mary's tone and went to where the old woman sat staring out into the street. Her talent as a reader worked on humans as well as folk, and she could see Mary was not only feeling down emotionally but physically too. The old woman had been a good friend of her grandmother, and now age was taking its toll. 'It's no trouble. I'm making some tea. Do you mind if I sit with you for a while?'

Mary frowned, her already wrinkled face crinkling further. 'Only if you have time.' The elderly woman didn't take her eyes from the street.

Nea pulled her ponytail undone and refastened it. 'No trouble at all. I want to hear about your adventures with Bess.'

After ducking back into the kitchen to make the tea, she soon found herself sitting across from the old woman and taking a bite of a cookie.

Mary sighed after taking a sip. 'You look so much like her.' She tilted her head to the side and studied Nea. With a definitive nod, she added, 'It's the way you smile. You have Gregor's blue eyes though. No mistaking them.'

'Grandpa misses her a lot. We all do.' Nea said in reply.

'I'll be joining her soon.'

Nea sighed, suddenly at a loss for words. It was true. Mary was going downhill pretty fast. There wasn't much she could do about it either. Her grandfather may have been able to slow his aging, but Mary Parsons was a human, non-folk, and there was nothing any of them could do. So she spent an hour with her grandmother's best friend, listening to the stories of the past before she headed out again.

Her next visit was to a middle-aged witch, who'd had her magic stilled because she wasn't able to control it anymore. Her house was small and disheveled, much like the witch herself.

'You again,' Pru Hepworth said when Nea came to

the door. 'Bringing more of your charity?' Her dark, tangled hair appeared to roil with anger.

Nea beamed a big smile. It was more like a shield against the cranky witch's spite. 'It's not charity. You contributed to the coven and now the coven owes you.'

Pru huffed and then stepped back to let her in. 'Your grandfather should have ended me,' she said as she followed Nea down the darkened hallway. 'Shouldn't have left me like this. Good for nothing ...'

Nea had heard this many times. Pru wasn't old as such but for some unknown reason her talent had started to fluctuate wildly. As this had been during a coven ritual, and someone had been badly hurt, Gregor, Nea's grandfather, had had no choice but to calm her talent until an answer could be found. Unfortunately, no solution had been discovered as yet, and the witch was in the depths of despair and liked to share her morose feelings about her predicament.

Nea's reading sense slipped easily into the other witch. While the surface of her emotions were aroused and swirling with feeling, beneath she was calm. She made a mental note to mention it to Gregor. Perhaps the problem was righting itself.

'As we've discussed before, it's temporary until the healers can work out the problem.'

'It's been six months.'

'I know,' she replied as she plonked the groceries and the books Pru had requested on the kitchen table, making room amongst the pile of letters and boxes and jars piled up there. 'I hope they come up with a solution soon.'

'Sure you do.' Pru's tone was harsh, like a whip.

Nea couldn't help reacting and swung around, her reply tumbling out of her. 'Of course I do. Do you think anyone enjoys the position that you are in?

That we don't feel for you? That we can't imagine what it must be like to be missing a part of yourself?'

The other witch's dark eyebrows rose, her hazel eyes rounded and her pale lips tightened.

Nea realized she had spoken out of turn. 'I'm sorry. I shouldn't have raised my voice. I—'

'No ... no ... you're right. I am feeling sorry for myself and a tad paranoid as well. Thank you for taking care of me. You are really very good to put up with me like you do.'

Nea patted her hand. 'Really it's a pleasure. I'll ask Gregor to come talk to you about progress. Okay?'

Pru's eyes lit up. 'Really? Thank you.'

She squeezed the older witch's hand. 'Of course, I will.' She checked the time on her phone. 'Look, I'd better go. I have some more errands to run.'

'Goodbye. Thank you and my regards to Gregor.'

She sat in the car, wondering if she should go back in and talk to the stilled witch some more. Losing her power was more than the other witch could bear. Her talent was integral to who she was and living without it wasn't much better than being dead. However, Gregor had asked her to visit a new family that had moved to the area so she didn't have time. She wanted to get to know the newcomers and tell them about the activities of the coven and also give them general information about the neighborhood.

Her phone buzzed, and on picking it up she saw there was a reminder to head over to another of the coven's older members in need of company and a good cup of tea.

Casting her gaze to the horizon, she realized it was getting late and she was running out of time. An hour and it would be dark. She turned the ignition on the car and drove off.

✿

The next morning, Grandpa Royston called up the stairs to where she checked her hair in the mirror. 'Bethanea, come and sit down. I want to have a word with you.'

It must be bad if he's using my full name. She pulled a face, making her freckled nose wrinkle. 'Coming,' she yelled, then checked her teeth before bounding down the stairs to see what he wanted.

'Oh? There you are,' he said as if surprised to see her. He was a big man, white blond hair and flashing, bright blue eyes.

Definitely something dodgy there. She bit her bottom lip. He was a powerful warlock so he knew where she was in the house and in the neighborhood, if truth be told—a fact she'd discovered after a few embarrassing moments when she was a teenager. Being caught half-naked with a member of the opposite sex was not a fond memory. As the boy had been human, it had been even more humiliating and devilishly hard to explain afterwards to either party.

'I've made you a nice cup of tea,' he said. 'Come sit in the living room.'

She followed behind Gregor Royston's large form. He was eighty-four but looked barely older than forty. A folk talent that he had in spades. She hoped she inherited a share of it. However, at the rate she got sunburned and freckled, she doubted that she had.

Her mother still looked young—not that she saw much of her. She'd gone off to Europe when Nea had been five years old. Anyway, it would just be her luck to take after the human side of the family.

She followed her grandfather and pulled up short. Her mouth dropped open, and she quickly shut it.

It was hard not to gape at what was before her. Her grandfather had brought out her grandma's old tea service and there were fresh scones on a tiered stand, with bowls of cream and jam to accompany them. She blinked, certain he hadn't baked them or conjured them, so he must have nipped to the bakery earlier. Her suspicion levels rose even higher. If there was a meter in her head, its pointer would be definitely in the red zone, flashing: *warning, warning. warning.*

Missing her moment to back out of the room and flee from the house, she moved to a chair. Blinking rapidly as she sat down, she took in the tea service that carried with it so many fond memories of her deceased grandmother. Bess had been human and an amazing woman. She'd captured the heart of a powerful warlock and he wouldn't give her up, no matter the consequences. So he'd married her in the human way and left the Sydney coven to form one of his own up here on the Central Coast.

What a life they had led. Bess had been a special woman—she'd had to be to manage a life with a warlock like Gregor—and had doted on Nea, her only granddaughter. Nea missed her deeply and she realized she always would. Bess had taken the place of her absent mother. She took comfort in the thought that Bess was a part of her and that her spirit and strength ran through her veins.

'What is it?' Gregor asked, taking in her look of utter surprise.

She closed her gaping mouth. 'Bess's tea service.' She indicated with her hand. Her grandfather had sideswiped her. Feeling emotional all of a sudden, she suppressed the tears. Tears would only upset the old man and there was no point in giving him a tactical advantage. This was an engagement of wills. He wanted something from her, badly.

'I wanted to add something to the occasion,' he said, his hand indicating the tea setting with a flourish.

'Occasion?' *Uh-oh.* 'What occasion?' She asked, not able to hide the suspicion in her voice.

He grinned. 'Just be patient. I'll get to that.'

He put the strainer on her cup and lifted the teapot. 'It's amazing how something like this—' He flicked the tip of the milk jug, with its gold rim and bright red rose pattern. '—an object, can invoke such memories.' He frowned. 'It doesn't get any easier, losing her, you know.'

'I know.'

He smiled at her, but the lift of his lips did not extinguish the sadness in his eyes. He'd done his best for his wife, using magic to preserve her looks and her health, but she'd faded suddenly and there was nothing that could have been done about it.

With a sigh, he lifted the pot and poured the tea. She took her cup. He levitated the tiered platter towards her. 'Scone?'

She surveyed the selection. 'I will.' *May as well take what's on offer. He's gone to a lot of trouble, after all.* She plucked one from the bottom tier, lavished it with jam and cream and then sat quietly in her chair and watched him serve himself.

The room was quiet and there was a kind of reverence building, as if Bess was there with them. Her mind calmed as she sipped the tea, savoring the richness of the blend. He let nothing show on his face, but a serenity emanated from him as he sipped tea and munched on his scone, deftly avoiding dropping dollops of cream into his plate.

After a few minutes, he sat back in his big recliner, a cup nestled in his hand. She took a bite of her scone and chewed, enjoying the tartness of the raspberry jam against the smooth richness of the whipped cream. One of Bess's homemade jams. This talk must be serious if he was dipping into his horde of preserves.

He jiggled the cup as he lowered it, making her look up. His white blond eyebrows shot up when he caught her eye. 'So, Nea. You've been hanging around the house a lot these last few months.'

She swallowed and lowered her eyelids. *Is this going to be the how's-your-love-life talk? Surely not.* He didn't need all this pomp to pry into her private life. He just had to bark at her and she'd answer.

'Is that a problem?' She kept house for him and loved being with him. He was so full of energy, and as he was the center of the coven, so was she. It was her life and she was content. Mostly content.

'No, no.' He spooned some cream onto another scone. 'Not a problem. Good actually, because I was wondering if you could do me a favor.'

Nea swallowed another mouthful, trying not to choke. 'Sure. What kind of favor?'

'I said to old Rory Penderton that I'd keep an eye on his boy, Drew.'

The bite of scone in her mouth was hard to swallow. She did her best and then cleared her throat. 'Well, you have been. He's visited here a few times.'

Her eyes narrowed at the memory of Drew. She'd never hit it off with the Sydney-based warlock who'd moved up here to the lake. She hadn't noticed his absence lately. Although, she noticed when he was around but for the wrong reasons. He put her instincts on alert.

'Yes, well ... now I'm worried about him. He's

been withdrawn, reclusive these last few weeks. I want to keep him involved with the coven and not with other influences.'

Her eyebrows rose. 'You mean with Pris Denholm, don't you?'

He lifted his head, his blue eyes piercing. 'What do you know?'

She shrugged. 'Not much, but folk talk. She's a dark witch, they say. And Elena's mother.' Elena had confided in her when they met, and it had seemed a bit sad that her mother didn't want to meet her own daughter. Particularly after abandoning her with humans as a baby. *Must be a real cow. Poor Elena.* Elena had married Jake Royston, her first cousin. At least her own mother communicated sometimes, when she had time to spare from her current brood. Ursula had left Riley, her father, to run off with a very flamboyant warlock from Spain. They had four children, none of whom she had seen. Riley had stayed to raise her, which she very much appreciated. However, he was often away too and currently with his girlfriend.

Gregor coughed and placed his tea cup back on the table next to his scone. 'I doubt either of them would benefit from you repeating that story about their connection.' He was as close to a glower as she'd ever seen him.

'You know I won't. So what's the problem?'

The snowy eyebrows lowered over his bright, blue eyes. 'Nothing. Of course you wouldn't say anything. I'm overreacting. I thought maybe you'd heard about Drew visiting Pris.'

She sat up straighter, rattling the cup in its saucer. 'Has he been visiting her?' she asked as she steadied the cup and placed it back on the table.

'I can't tell. He's shielded himself from my sight.'

Her eyes narrowed. 'Does he have the talent for

that?' As she'd not taken an interest in Drew other than politeness, due to her role as the granddaughter of the head of the coven and keeper of his house, she knew next to nothing about the surly warlock's abilities. Although she was a reader and generally couldn't help detecting something on the surface layers of the people she met, she'd gotten nothing from Drew, and as he didn't rate further in her interest, she'd not bothered thinking anything about it. *Shielding himself from Grandpa! That is interesting.* It went without saying that he'd shielded from her, too. She chewed her bottom lip. It wasn't good she hadn't picked up on that. She should have noticed the shielding. It meant there was more work to be done on honing her talent.

Gregor eased into the recliner, letting out a huge sigh. For the first time, she got a sense of his real age. He was tired, tired in the heart. His grief had not left him. If anything he clung to it, like a baby to a comforter. For a short time, it was right and natural for him to grieve, but if it went on much longer, she'd be concerned.

'To tell the truth, I'm not sure,' he said, continuing the conversation. 'He's never let me assess him, and his father mentioned that he was good at hiding parts of himself. He could be shielding himself or it could be her doing it for him.'

Her. The dark witch. Someone they didn't like to think about.

'So what can I do?' she asked, leaning forward to plop a large dollop of jam on the second half of her scone. She thought she knew what was coming, but she wanted her grandfather to spell it out. No volunteering for chores, particularly disagreeable ones. She'd fallen far too often for those without putting up a fight.

He met her gaze. 'I thought maybe you could take him out, entertain him.'

'Entertain him? How?' She narrowed her eyelids, letting him know quite plainly she was suspicious.

He picked up his tea, took a sip and swallowed. 'You know.' He shrugged. 'Take him on a date.'

She stilled, the cream dropping from her scone to plop on the plate. 'You can't be serious.' Her cheeks burned and she had to put her plate down in case she broke it.

The old man squirmed on his chair. 'Well, it was an … idea.'

She took in a few deep breaths, anchoring herself. 'But you wouldn't want me to get serious with him, would you?' She couldn't hide the incredulity of her voice. *Drew Penderton is a good-looking creep. Scratch that. I should be more charitable. An asshole with grooming, or better still, a pretty face with a sour-grape constitution. Wow! Where did that come from?* She gaped, appalled at the strength of her ill feeling.

He tilted his head. 'That would be entirely up to you. He needs a connection to the coven and so far he's made none. A romance might give him an incentive. The poor boy has tried to—'

She wasn't having any of that nonsense. 'No, he hasn't. He's been a right bastard to anyone who's tried to be nice. He's good-looking, but Prince Charming he's not.'

Gregor raised a defensive hand. 'Now, Nea …'

'Don't you "now Nea" me. Romance? With Drew Penderton! Why, he laughed at my freckles and then called me moonface.' *Moonface? The pig!* The scone was like a lump of lead in her stomach. She took some more tea, scalding her tongue. Her heart raced and she sucked in big breaths.

Gregor's eyes widened when he saw her agitation.

'So he's a little churlish.' He smiled and relaxed back into his chair. 'Don't take it to heart. He just needs a bright young thing to help him find his way.'

She sensed that her grandfather was using his power to calm her down and soothe her. While she was aware of it, she didn't fight it but put her cup on the tray and slid her plate under it. 'I find it very hard to shine around him. He oppresses me. Not his type.'

He pursed his lips, regarded her for a few moments, and then started packing the dishes onto a tray. 'How do you know until you try?' he ventured, this time not exerting his influence.

She picked up the tray that was now full of their tea things and stood. She wasn't going to budge. He stood too and grabbed the tray, holding her still. 'Please,' he said softly, reasonably.

She looked down, letting her hair cover half her face. She chewed her bottom lip. *What could it hurt? Just one date. Gregor can't expect more. It will make him so happy, take away some of his worry. It is such a small thing.*

She grinned and met his concerned eyes. 'Look, I'll contact him and see if he wants to do something. If he does, we can take it from there. But that's it. I'm not going to chase him down for a date.'

Gregor grinned. He took the tray from her, and she rescued the tiered platter as it wobbled. She followed him out to the kitchen. He said over his shoulder, 'I appreciate it. If you get a chance to read him, then do?'

'Without his permission?' She put the platter on the bench next to the sink.

He nodded. 'More to the point, without him knowing.'

She took the teapot and tipped out the dregs into the bench top compost bin. 'I think you overestimate my talent, Grandpa.' She soothed her fingers over the teapot and sighed, thinking of her grandmother.

'Don't call me Grandpa. It ages me. Call me Gregor, like everyone else does.'

She gazed up at him, meeting his bright blue eyes. 'I miss her.'

He looked down, and picked up a cup and stared at it. 'I do too. It makes me sad that the talent I have and cherish is the one thing that separated us. Nothing else did, you know.'

'Do you regret leaving the other coven to be with her?'

He looked at her hard in the eye. 'No, never!' He lowered the teacup onto the bench and his gaze focused somewhere else. 'It was hard starting from scratch up here. Lake Macquarie was a backwater then. We aren't as big or as rich as the Sydney coven, but it's been good. Bess was happy here. Our sons were, too, in their younger days.'

She sighed with a touch of envy. 'You gave her a good life. You shared so many beautiful moments. I'm beginning to despair of finding such love that you two had.'

His shoulders sagged. 'You spend too much time looking after me and the house.' He placed the dishes in the sink and then turned to her. 'You should get out more, maybe go to Sydney and spend time with Jake and Elena.'

She laughed. 'I did go to Sydney. Remember? I babysat for a while. I love being there with them, but if it's a Sydney warlock you have in mind I don't fancy my chances. Man shortage and all that. Some of the witches down there talked to me at social events but only because I'm too plain to be competition.' She tapped her nose full of freckles. 'Grace and

Elena call them bitch-witches, you know.' She let out a laugh.

His brow furrowed, sending his white eyebrows knitting together. 'Well, further afield then. Britain or Europe?'

She picked up a tea towel and paused. 'But I thought you were concerned about the dark uprisings there.'

He cocked his head to the side. 'I am, but I'm sure you would be safe. They are localized to particular areas. Just avoid those.'

'You going to pay my fare I suppose in return for my little favor?' She grinned at him cheekily. She didn't want to leave the lake or Gregor permanently, even though it lowered her chances of finding someone suitable. But a nice expenses-paid jaunt might be just the trick to improve her chances.

'You make it sound like a transaction.' He grunted. 'It's not. You've been looking after me and deserve a break. Not that I don't appreciate it.'

She patted him on the arm. 'You don't need to bribe me. I'll check Drew out; if there's a spark there I'm happy to see where it leads.' Personally, she doubted there would be, but she was happy enough to give it a try. Maybe things would improve on their third or was it fourth acquaintance. She'd nothing to lose except time and maybe her temper.

Her grandfather reached over and clasped her hand. 'Just be careful. Now clear off. I want to take care of this.' He started to prepare the dishes for washing up in the human way. He didn't like wasting magic on frivolous things.

As her gaze lingered, she noticed his expression was sad. He looked like he was one with his memories, but there was something else, something bothering him, something he wasn't talking about. She hadn't known him to be secretive before. She tried to sense where his anxiety was coming from but the old man was sealed up tight. A good precaution with a reader in the house.

'Okay. I'm going for a walk and then I'll see what Drew is up to.'

The sun had just set on the western side of the lake and dusk embraced them. Nea walked with Drew on the tail end of a rather irritating date. A walk along the shore was usually a cure-all—the light breeze shredding dark moods and dissipating low spirits. Right then, she was too tense to relax.

'So you think hanging around the lake is fun?' Drew Penderton asked, with a sneer evident in his voice. He swiped at some long grass, cutting off the tips.

She exhaled loudly. 'Yes, I do. But I was brought up here. I like this space, the lake, the quiet life. Not as sophisticated or as exciting as Sydney, I know.'

Drawing closer to the water, the young warlock bent down and picked up a stone. He pitched it and then she detected a slight vibration as he used his talent to make it skip and skip until it passed out of sight. 'This place has nothing on Sydney.'

The moon rose and silver light glittered over the lake's surface. The lunar energy tickled along the bare skin of her arms. 'Isn't there anything you like about the place?'

'Some things. Too many humans though for my taste.' He faced her, but his expression was bland and muted by shadow. She couldn't pick up anything from the exterior of him. It was as blank as his inner landscape. *Or was that a desolate inner landscape?*

He glanced at the moon, and she took the opportunity to read him but came up against a wall. It had been that way at dinner. Stifled conversation—like trying to converse through the gap in a paling fence. She could read nothing. His mind was hidden by a steel shutter. She'd never come across someone like that. Not even surface thoughts. Even his gestures were subdued. He could be having a fab time or totally hating every moment. She couldn't even interpret his body language. That swept her up on a wave of uncertainty. Most people, including the folk, leaked something. As he gave off nothing, it was very hard to like him or even establish empathy with him.

He walked ahead, then stopped and half-turned. 'You finished your inspection?'

She frowned. While she had detected nothing, he'd obviously sensed her light reading probe. 'I'm a reader. It comes with the territory. But I can't sense anything.'

He lifted his chin as he nodded. 'Good.'

'How do you do that? You know, hide what you're thinking and feeling?'

'Maybe I'm not. Maybe you're useless.'

'Maybe,' she replied and shrugged. *What a brute!*

He moved ahead of her and paused to look back. 'Coming?'

The path ahead was overshadowed by trees, blocking out the moonlight. She hesitated. 'It's dark. I don't think …' She didn't know why it bothered her, but her anxiety had been building all evening.

'We'll be on the road soon. Plenty of light then.'

Her witch sense tingled, and she sent out her talent. There was something not right ahead. 'Where are we going?'

'Nowhere in particular," he replied, giving nothing away.

She paused and looked in the other direction. 'In that case, can we go the other way?'

Suddenly he was there, his fingers gripping her elbow. 'No, I want to go this way.' His voice held command.

Shaking off the magic he'd thrown at her, perhaps unwittingly, she gaped down at the offending hand. 'Let me go. You're hurting me.'

A growl slipped past his gritted teeth. There was something feral and wild in his expression. Alarm pulsed through her. He didn't let her go, and his grip tightened.

'Drew!' He didn't seem to hear her. 'Let. Me. Go!' she yelled into his face.

Still no reaction from him—just that expression and the dark pull of his eyes.

She shoved him back with a burst of magic, an instinctive push. His fingers released and a yell escaped him. He staggered away, blinked, and shook his head. Righting himself, he gaped at her, dumbfounded. 'What the fuck? Why did you do that?'

'Sorry!' She was appalled at what she'd done. A human would have sustained an injury. 'You were hurting me.'

He looked down at his hands. 'Was I?'

'Yes,' she said as she rubbed the spot where his fingers had dug in.

He stared at her, his head tilted to one side. 'You're quite strong for a little thing. I didn't realize.'

She panted, her heart thumping. She hadn't known she had it in her. Repulsion and striking was something that she'd never used much at all. Hadn't needed to. Still on guard, she stared at him. Tentatively, she reached out to skim his inner landscape but there was still nothing. His emotions—she doubted he had any—were sealed up tight.

He moved towards her.

'Stay back,' she commanded in a clear and loud voice, fists clenched at her side.

He paused and spread his hands. A fleeting smile did wonders for his features. 'I didn't mean to hurt you.' He shrugged as if her aversion didn't matter. 'There's a house I want to show you. No big deal. We won't go in, not if you don't want to.'

She breathed deeply, her panic receding. She was a big girl, a smart witch. Surely she was a match for Drew, and besides, her grandfather wanted to know what he was up to. She hated letting her grandfather down. Talking with Drew hadn't shed any light on anything to do with his life, his motivations or activities. Reading him had revealed nothing. This was an opportunity to see what interested him and maybe then get some inkling about what he really thought and felt. She nodded, relaxing her fists, not realizing she had been poised ready for attack. 'Sure. I'll come along.'

A vagrant thought tempted her to hail Gregor—to communicate her alarm. Drew would detect that and right now, she wanted to pursue this moment with him. Now he knew she wasn't a pushover, maybe he'd respect her more ... open up. *Long shot!*

The young warlock stepped back and let her precede him, then he joined her on the path. 'So what have you been doing with yourself since you've been up here?' she asked conversationally, as if they hadn't been engaging in magical fisticuffs.

'You already asked me that.'

She laughed it off. 'I did, but you didn't say. Are you working for a spy agency or something? Is that why you won't talk about it? Is it a national secret?'

'It's none of your business,' he snapped at her, his voice hard.

Woah! She sighed low and long. 'Geez, Drew, trying to get to know you is like trying to understand what the moon is thinking. Don't you know it's how folk converse? I tell you a bit about me, you tell me a bit about you ...'

'I don't want to do what others do. I want to be left alone.'

'Do you? Just a minute ago you didn't want me to leave. That's rather contradictory.'

His dark gaze passed over her. 'It's complicated.'

She chuckled and kicked a twig out of her way as they headed up the hill. They walked in silence for a few minutes more. Goosebumps erupted on her arms. Something very creepy existed nearby. It was like walking across a cemetery where the spirits were unsettled. 'It can't be that complicated. Why do you want me here with you?'

'Maybe I want to rape you.' He gestured to the bush around him. 'It's quiet here. No one will see, or hear you scream or anything. I can do it before anyone comes and finds you—what's left of you, that is.'

She stopped in her tracks, her skin chilled. He knew she could fight him off. 'Is that your idea of a joke?'

'Maybe.' His dark eyes glittered as they met hers.

'That's not even funny.'

He grinned at her. 'Maybe not. Surely it's no surprise. Didn't Elena tell you what happened?'

'Elena? Your half-sister?' She was puzzled. *What did he mean? Had he raped his half-sister, attacked her?*

'Yeah, but I didn't know she was my sister at the time.'

Her heart rate kicked up. Dread washed over her. Maybe he wasn't joking, and that was unnerving.

'She's not said anything to me about you.'

He began walking again. 'I don't mind if you hail your grandfather and tell him exactly where you are. I know you want to.'

'You can read me?' That surprised and worried her.

'I don't have to. You're so jittery, it makes sense. I know you only asked me out because he asked it as a favor.'

She narrowed her gaze, assessing him. Maybe she was jittery, but if he was guessing it was so close to the truth it was scary. If he could read her, she needed to do more work on her shielding, because a leaky mind was not a good look. *Great. This date has been a huge mistake.*

She shot Gregor a tight hail along the lines of: *Total disaster. At creepy place, near Catherine Hill Bay. Come for me.* Her grandfather replied that he was on his way.

'You know, Drew. You aren't helping yourself. You'd get on better with folk if you were more open.'

'I'm doing fine. You think I want sex from the likes of you? You're wrong. I'm kept well satisfied.'

'Really? How? Masturbation?' She knew all about that. Blokes took themselves in hand.

The feral snarl was back. 'Shut up, bitch. I get all the sex I want.' He rolled his shoulders, and his fists clenched by his sides. 'Great sex. Powerful sex. Better than you or any other witch your age could offer.'

There was a fever brewing in his eyes. It was the first hint of emotion she'd seen from him. He'd lifted the hatches on his mind. She looked deep and gasped.

Festering anger. Swirling malice. Throbbing emotional pain. Fear of rejection. Loneliness. Then a red spear of something alien lashing out.

A knife of pain pierced her brain. Staggering back, she shook her head. She winced, wiping at her now watering eyes. 'Goddess! That hurt.'

'Don't pry,' he snapped and then turned away, his shoulders hunched.

Blinking, she reached out tentatively. What she'd detected was hidden now, but she'd tasted enough to know Gregor's fears were justified. Something powerful lurked in this strange warlock's mind amongst the detritus of his emotional landscape.

'Sorry,' she said. 'It was instinctive.' She rubbed her forehead, trying to erase the dull ache.

He strode away from her and she followed, walking into a tree tunnel, where the intertwined branches overhead blocked out the moonlight.

Alone with him in the dark, her skin broke out in a sweat and her breath hitched on an inhale, as if she'd been chilled to her soul. Maybe it wasn't a good idea to be out here with him. Fear eroded her earlier confidence. Yet, Gregor was on his way, so she calmed her nerves.

The path they trod narrowed down to dirt. Leaves and branches grabbed at her. Frogs chirped and the wind in the trees slapped leaves together. A cobweb kissed her face and she shuddered, using her talent to repel any spiders.

They kept walking, she just trailed behind with nothing but the night for a cloak.

Suddenly, they were out onto a normal street, with a sidewalk and a bitumen road. A lone street-light cast a feeble glow over an intersection. Low mist draped over the road and collected around a ruin of a house made up of a few supporting stumps, one wall just a frame of rotting wood. It had no roof, but rubble decorated the ground between the clumps of weeds.

Next to it was another house, an old two-level Victorian weatherboard that had once been grand, but appeared rundown, abandoned. Gables sagged, and its balcony just clung to the edifice, assisted by a tenacious ivy vine. The lower veranda was decorated in rubbish: an old couch, a bicycle wheel, a wicker pram, and a pile of rags sagging through a split in a rubbish bag.

'That's what you wanted me to see, isn't it?' She chewed her bottom lip and swept her hair out of her eyes. It was very odd and unsettling. *Why here? What does Drew want with this place?*

He turned to the house and put his hands on his hips. 'Maybe. Maybe not. I don't think you're quite ready for it yet.'

'Ready for what—a tour of a haunted house?' She tried not to laugh. It seemed so childish and added to her confusion about him.

Nevertheless, she let her talent run free, trying to find the source of her unease with her reading skill. The ruin was a sad place, full of grief with under-tones of suffering and death. Her talent swept over the old house next to it and elicited a shiver up her spine. Something very bad had happened there. It was much worse than the ruin. It leaned over the re-mains of the other house as if it fed off the vibrations emanating from it.

She sent her talent lower, to the foundations, and there was nothing to sense. It was a blank space, pos-sibly blocked. She switched back to the ruin, and her other sight sunk into the ground. There she could read the memory of the earth, the blood and the tears that had dripped down to soak into the dirt. It reeked of death. Yet, there was something there, something that quivered when her talent passed over it. Her talent went back to that spot seeking, probing and prodding, like it was a blind pimple emerging on her chin.

She poked at it. The quiver became a kindled flame, as if she'd woken something that had lain quiescent for an age. She didn't like the sensation, the questing tendrils that seemed ravenous and all too eager, and instinctively pulled her talent back. The thing she disturbed grew stronger, tried to latch on, tried to follow. That wasn't meant to happen. Her talent wasn't meant to disturb, only to read, like a soft wind gently teasing. She dared not send her talent back for a second read. She hoped whatever it was would sink back down in the dark earth, would go back to sleep and lie quietly as if she'd never disturbed it.

'Let's keep walking,' she said, unable to dampen her fearful response. *What is this place? What is that sensation of something coming alive at the touch of my mind?* It hadn't quieted. No, it was like a kindled flame in the dark, burning brighter with every breath she took.

'Why? What's your hurry? The night is young.' Drew laughed, but it was an ugly sound with no joy in it. Just dead. She shivered at the thought, rubbing at her upper arms.

Did he know what lay in the ruin? Was that why he'd brought her here? Was this some secret she had to uncover, some game that had to be played?

She couldn't help herself. It was like trying not to pick at a scab. She sent her talent back again, straight to the spot where something moved, something living so close to death it may as well be dead.

The flame of its essence surged brighter—touched

her talent tentatively, then suddenly latched on, like a leach sucking, sucking. Her eyes widened. She clawed in a breath and reeled in her talent. The presence flared and expanded.

Her instinct was to bolt, and she didn't realize she'd started to until Drew put his hand out and stopped her. 'What is it?' he asked. 'Chicken?'

She wasn't about to tell him. She shook her head, mute.

'Come on. What gives?' He faced the ruin. She couldn't detect his use of talent so didn't know if he sensed that thing growing more alert with each breath.

Maybe he already knew what it was. Maybe that was why he'd brought her there.

She wanted to put some distance between herself and the creepy warlock and his penchant for eerie ruins, but he closed in.

'Gregor ... is ... is ... coming ...' She was hardly able to breathe. Sweat broke out on her forehead.

He chuckled, the sound opposite of mirth. 'The sight of a haunted house is enough to rattle you. Excellent.' His laugh was the inside of a fire pit where all the oxygen had been sucked out. He drew her to him, one arm around her back, and in her fright she didn't resist. He leaned over her as he tilted her back, a parody of romance. With his eyebrows arched in mockery, he leaned his face close. 'Want to fuck?'

It was the bucket of cold water she needed. His words, so emotionlessly uttered, were as inviting as jumping into the jaws of a shark. *Hell no!* She pulled herself together using indignation to sweep away the last of her fear. She closed her mind to what she had sensed and resisted the urge to belt him across the mouth. 'No. Definitely not,' she spat.

He sneered and righted her. His dark eyes reflected the light from the streetlamp, yet his expression was set into muted lines. She shook her head as he stepped away and tugged his sweater over the waist of his jeans.

'You know, I've had better offers.' She said lightly to hide her indignation.

'I'm willing to lower my standards,' he said, trying to smirk and failing, his expression closer to a sneer.

'I'm not,' she replied. *That desperate!*

'How do you know until you try? Sex is mechanical. You make too much of it.'

With her hands on her hips, she seared him with a look. 'Sex is not just mechanical to me. You'd have to do more than blank yourself; you'd have to talk to me to make me want to share myself with you, make a connection mentally, emotionally. I need to be able to read you, to understand you and trust you to get intimate. That's not happening for me. Think about it, and if you're willing to be open, we can try again sometime.' *Over my dead body.*

He sneered. 'You're such a hypocrite. You're just as closed as me.'

She backed away. Gregor was close now; she could sense him drawing near. She'd be rescued soon. 'That's just plain weird. I'm not closed. I've been open the whole evening. Surely you can read me.' She tugged on her hair. 'Maybe you can't understand what you read.'

His face was impassive but there was a hard glint in his eyes.

Then it twigged. 'Is that it? You have no empathy?'

The slap came out of nowhere. She reeled and her hand went to her cheek, the flesh a stinging throb. 'What the hell?'

The blandness of him had ripened into raw anger.

She saw it in the flush of his cheeks and the slant of his mouth.

'Shut the fuck up. Don't you dare judge me.'

'I wasn't. I didn't. I'm just trying to understand—' Reaction set in—her hands trembled. He'd hit her. Drew Penderton had hit her. Just like that. She was so shocked and scared, she didn't even think of hexing him. For the first time in her life someone had assaulted her.

Gregor's car skidded to a stop. Neither of them turned towards it, their gazes locked on each other. Her heart thumped. Something about Drew scared her to her core. 'Run, little mouse, little freckled moonface. I've got a real woman, a woman with power. Don't need to do anything to impress her.'

She backed up to the car, nodding. Her cheek smarted and her eyes watered, but she wasn't about to let him see that he'd hurt her. She'd obtained the information Gregor wanted. The woman with power had to be Pris. Gregor wasn't going to like it, but she considered it was too late to do anything about it. The strangeness that was Drew Penderton had morphed into something else. If he'd been twisted before, he was a damned pretzel now. He was dangerous.

The passenger door swung open, and backing away, she bumped her rear against it.

'Nea?' Her grandfather called out.

She didn't trust Drew so kept facing him in case he hexed her. If she shielded, Gregor would intervene. It could get messy.

Gregor was there to protect her so she calmed down. She was safe now. She suspected that Drew had let out more than he'd intended and that her insight about his lack of empathy had touched a raw nerve.

Breaking eye contact with Drew, she took her

chance and jumped into the car. 'It's okay. Just drive.' She tugged the door shut.

Gregor did a double-take. 'What happened?'

Her hand went to her smarting cheek. She didn't realize the injury would be obvious.

'Did he hit you?" Gregor exploded and gripped the steering wheel. " I'll squash him.'

She touched his hand. 'No, just drive. Please.'

'Nea?' His eyes were large and angry. His power bristled beneath the surface.

'Just take me home. There's no point. Just go.'

Looking out the window she saw Drew standing under the streetlight, his face cast in eerie shadow, looking more like a ghoul than a man. She hugged herself and closed her eyes, blocking out the sight of him.

Gregor turned the wheel and took off, at first muttering to himself, then he started swearing up a storm.

She touched his arm again. 'Don't hex him. Just leave it.'

Gregor gripped the wheel. 'I'm sorry. It's my fault. I shouldn't have asked you. Should've known he was some kind of mongrel.'

She glanced back as they turned the corner. The strange warlock was no longer standing there.

'How could you know that? You were only trying to do your best, your duty as leader of the coven. So was I. He's so ... so ... unreadable ... so unreachable.'

'You're not hurt?'

She shook her head. 'Taken by surprise is all.'

Gregor sighed, clicked the indicator and then turned onto the main road. 'You say he's unreadable. So you can't tell what he's been up to?'

'More than unreadable. He doesn't give anything away, no expression, except the sneer. No body language. I couldn't tell if he hates me or is madly in love with me. Although I could guess. Anyway it was downright unnerving.'

'So you couldn't find out anything?'

'Only what he wanted to tell me and maybe a bit more than he intended.'

'And that is?'

'He's sleeping with an older, more experienced, woman, I think, and judging from what he said, a woman with power. Before that, just for a moment I caught a glimpse of something. It struck at me.' She touched her forehead where that malicious strike had hit. 'He's into something dark. Something dangerous.' She let out a sigh. 'He likes it.'

'Hmmm.' Her grandfather's eyebrows were drawn down so low it was a wonder he could see to drive. He turned another corner and the rear driver's side tyre hit the curb, making the car jerk. Maybe those eyebrows were impeding his vision after all.

She folded her arms and glared out the window. 'My thoughts exactly.'

'It does seem that he's mixed up with the dark witch.' He slapped the steering wheel. 'I failed, just like before.'

'What?'

'Nothing.'

'But you just said like before. What's that about?'

'Nothing to interest you. Ancient history, before you were born,' he said gruffly.

'So tell me ...'

He stared out the windscreen and gripped the wheel. For a minute, she thought he wasn't going to answer. Then he spoke. 'I've lost young warlocks to Pris before. In the early days of the coven.'

'Oh, but you have an agreement with her.' She regarded him as he concentrated on the road.

'We do now. Have done for many years. Someone like Drew, though, without a connection to us, is fair game.' He flicked her a glance. 'So any hope of reaching him, steering him away from this course in your opinion?'

Shaking her head, she answered, 'I don't know. He's so closed. I don't see how he could have sex with anyone, dark witch or otherwise. It's such a turn-off. Tonight was even worse than other times I've met him and tried to make conversation. It was so much hard work. He's got talent, lots of it, but it's locked away behind a shield of steel.'

'He hit you.' He clenched his jaw. 'I'm not happy to let that lie. I can't let that go unpunished.'

'Yes, he did, but leave it. I hit a nerve. I said he didn't have empathy and he reacted.'

'But that's not on, Nea. You can't accept that behavior. As your grandfather, as the head of the coven, I can't either.'

'Look, he caught me by surprise. Although now I come to think of it, he was rather surly so I should have been wise to it. Maybe that's what appeals to dark witches: nastiness and a bad temper.'

Gregor grunted. It was as close to a laugh as she was going to get from him. She didn't want him going after Drew. Just the thought filled her with foreboding. Maybe that was what Drew was after. Provoke Gregor, weaken the coven and then ... and then what? She couldn't imagine why or what he'd do if it did come to that.

'Do you know he asked if Elena had said something about him? Did she?'

'Elena? In what context?'

'He ... um ...' She scrunched up her nose, wondering if she should tell him about that disturbing conversation.

'Nea...' His voice held warning. 'Tell me—no hedging.'

'Okay. She came up in a conversation about rape.'

He squeezed the steering wheel and his knuckles went white and then missed the turnoff to their street. 'Shit!' He hit the steering wheel. 'What conversation?'

'Grandpa ... just let it lie now. I want to forget the whole thing.'

'I'll speak to Jake and then Elena. I want the truth.' After taking the next turnoff, he finally pulled into their driveway. The exterior lights were on and the front door swung open.

When she stepped inside, he drew her into a bear hug and kissed her cheek. 'I'm sorry, my darling girl.'

'It's not your fault,' she said as he released her. 'You know, I pity him. I sense he can never know love and that's a crying shame.'

'Yes, I feel for him too.'

'Is that a bath running?'

Her grandfather smiled and nodded. He must have been upset; he'd used his talent for something trivial. 'Yes, now come here and let me look at your face.' After staring at her for a minute or so he sent some healing into her cheek.

She heard her grandpa sigh as she went upstairs to take her bath. It sounded like he was giving up, and that was the saddest sound she'd ever heard.

The presence rippled and stirred, wisps of itself stretching out tentatively, learning the extent of its existence. If bones could creak, his would have. If there were breath in his lungs, he would have yawned. He'd been asleep for so long. Dormant. Alone. Desolate.

Awakened by the talent that trailed like soft feathers across his substance, he was hungry for more. The mind behind the talent was warm, vibrant, alive. It excited his appetite. It stirred his curiosity. It made him want to live. It was a bright light that drew him from the darkness and spiraled into him, setting him afire.

With her was another presence—dark, unexciting. He'd had enough of the dark and pain and abandonment. What was he doing with such a light one? Surely his night would extinguish her day.

Protective feelings sprang awake in his soul. That couldn't happen. He wouldn't let that beautiful light die.

He thought back to that moment of touch when her light essence had caressed him, so sweetly and subtly that he could have wept, if only he had eyes, or tears.

The lake lapped at the shore nearby, its suppressed essence like an unripe thundercloud. The moon's feeble energy flitted across the earth, unable to penetrate deeply to where he lay. He'd have to rise up to taste it and even then he would have to find some life force to stir, to bring his essence forth. He sent out questing threads to the land nearby, detecting small creatures, their energy like little glowing gems. They came towards him, drawn by his vibrations. Soon, he would be able to free himself.

CHAPTER THREE

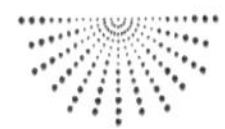

Nea's shift on the fishing boat drew to a close. She said farewell to the fishermen, stored the boat gear, stacked the cooling bin with the perishables for the skipper, Matt, and mopped the deck. Gregor had dropped her off that morning and rather than bother her grandfather for a lift home, she decided to walk. It was a great excuse not to be carrying any fish.

'You sure you don't want some?' Matt asked again as he clicked the remote on his ute. He had quite a stack in his little cooler.

'I'm walking. Can't. Too heavy. But thanks anyhow.'

'No problems. See you later then. I'll call you when I get the next tour up.'

She waved goodbye and headed along the road. The sun was low, skimming the surface of the lake with silver and pink. Some of the white clouds were tinged with grey.

A man dressed in jeans, with his hands in his pockets, leant against a light pole. She checked him out, relieved it wasn't Drew. This man was tall, olive-skinned, with longish hair that curled along the edges of his collar and face. She'd not seen him around before.

There was something easy and familiar about him. He nodded as he caught her eye. 'Good day out?' he asked, breaking into a stunning smile.

She slowed and looked back at the boat. Matt was still there, loading his ute. He waved at her. She turned back to the man. 'It was. You new around here?' She was trying hard not to read him. She wanted to enjoy the moment, enjoy meeting someone without the disappointment of knowing he or she was thinking about the smallness of her boobs, or her freckles, or the itch in his or her butt.

His hazel eyes glowed. 'I grew up around here. It's great to be back. The name is Earl, by the way.'

She smiled, nodding slightly. 'Earl. Nice name. My name is Bethanea, but my friends call me Nea.'

A grin altered his face, and her eyes were drawn to its handsome lines and the warm light in his eyes. *Damn he's good-looking. I'm melting.*

'May I call you Nea?' he asked.

'Yes, of course.' She needed to keep moving, juggling the urge to flirt and the need not to appear too keen. 'I've got to head off now. But maybe I'll see you around.'

'Yes, I'll see you around.' His smile lingered on her until she turned away.

She kept walking, all the while resisting the impulse to look back and read Earl. Part of her wanted to enjoy the package at face value—a handsome man who had noticed her—rather than seeing deeper and being disappointed.

As she headed up the road near the park, dark gray clouds roiled, bringing more than a hint of rain. Pausing, she looked over her shoulder, but Earl was nowhere to be seen. It was odd, because no cars had driven off. Matt's ute was still visible by the jetty. Maybe the handsome dude lived nearby.

With a sigh, she kept on walking, past oversized houses with huge entertainment decks that hungered for views across the lake. Some had boats moored at private jetties. Many were holiday houses, others were filled with retirees from Sydney, and a few were occupied by locals who'd been born and bred in this space, as she had been.

As she passed the manicured gardens and inhaled the scent of saltwater, she wondered about her life. Recently, her grandfather had been encouraging her to expand her horizons, find a life for herself. Yet, she was perfectly content living with him and doing those little things for the folk in the coven. The prospects in the romance department weren't that good locally. Going away permanently would mean giving her grandfather up, and she didn't want that. In her heart she knew she couldn't set up house away from this place, away from all the other people she cared about.

With a sense of guilt, she realized she didn't use her talent to its full. Since hearing that Declan Mallory had a school for teaching battle skills, the thought had crossed her mind that she should try her hand at that, or at something else. Yet, joining the Sydney coven seemed to be a betrayal of her grandfather and all that he had fought for. The Sydney coven had changed its ways since he'd left and they were on good terms but still ...

Breathing in the moist lake air, she experienced a thrill and knew that she didn't want to leave. Didn't want to change anything. Except maybe getting a sex life.

With a laugh at herself, she mused over her limited options. Most warlocks in the area were taken, or like Drew—not worth having. Maybe she should just marry a human and forget about her talent, about that other life. She'd known other folk who'd done that. They blended in, they forgot, and they got on with their lives.

Making a decision like that was way too hard. It would break her grandfather's heart. Gregor needed her and she needed him. At twenty-two, it was early days, so she shouldn't be sweating it. Who knew what chance would throw her way?

She remembered the first time she'd met Jake, and how much finding out he was a warlock with talent had changed his life. She sighed. Maybe that was when her unsettled feelings had started. He and Elena were amazing to see together. The thought she wouldn't have a match like that haunted her.

The absence of intimacy in her life was like a persistent ache that could be sublimated at times, but never forgotten. To kiss, to caress—there was no joy greater, particularly if one cared, one loved. She'd had her crushes in her teens, but the well had been dry these last few years. She didn't want to be desperate, but she couldn't help wondering if this was what her life was going to be. If this was all it was meant to be.

The soles of her sandals slapped her heels as she walked along the footpath. A sudden sharp pain meant she had to stop and dig a stone out from between her toes. The cool evening settled around her with the brush of night growing thicker with the minutes. Restless birds chattered and squawked as they readied their perches for the coming night. Damp air brushed against the bare skin of her legs.

Rather than taking the bicycle path through the dark bush, she chose to follow the road that skirted Sunshine Park. Although she was able to take care of herself, she'd rather not court problems by walking alone among the trees and scrub.

Still, even though she kept to the road, the trees blocked out the dusk, making it darker than she liked. There were no streetlights, just the occasional golden glow from houses across the road, which were set far back so not very illuminating.

After walking for ten minutes or so, she began to feel edgy. It was her witchsense again. Something jangled her nerves, sent her thoughts keening. Bracing her arms around herself, she rubbed at the gooseflesh on her skin as she slowed and looked for the source of her unease. It wasn't cold. The night was sultry, yet she was chilled.

Stopping in her tracks, a sudden silence made her heart flutter. Her senses picked up nothing: no animals scurrying in the undergrowth, no lovers coupling or even holding hands, no insects or birds nesting. It was dead. There was an impenetrable wall around her. Only her eyes could see. For all she could sense, she was the only person in the world. A creeping feeling tickled the back of her neck. There was something in the park. It blocked out everything.

A wall of malevolence built around her. It had a familiar tang. 'Drew,' she whispered and backed away.

Quickly assessing her options, she discarded running to the nearest house. They couldn't help her. Questing out with her senses, she tried to hail Gregor but she couldn't cleave the silence around her. The cloying nothingness scared her to her soul. A scream built in her throat.

Drowning in the still emptiness surrounding her, she reached for a calm place within herself. She was better than this. She had strength and skill, and Gregor had taught her well. While she couldn't detect the edges of the wall pressing down on her, she knew it had limits. She kept walking, then burst into a trot. The dark wall still surrounded her, thick and black. She ran faster, testing the edges of it, looking for cracks. There was a streetlight up ahead. Not far to her home. The thought of Gregor being there for her renewed her strength.

Stopping suddenly, she flung out a spear of talent. The wall shuddered, the fabric of it thinning. She feinted somewhere else, knowing that whoever it was would need to strengthen the wall there. Quickly, she was back at the weak spot, tearing through it. She sensed rather than heard the wall shatter.

Panting, she ran the last stretch to the corner of her street. Then, slowing down, she caught her breath, looking behind her and seeing nothing but the houses and the trees swaying softly. She could almost think that she'd imagined it.

Inside, Gregor sat in his easy chair. 'Matt said you were walking home. I was getting worried.'

'Worried? Why? Did you detect something?'

Does he know? Is he alert to something going on?

He shrugged. 'No particular reason.'

She read the holding back. Not quite a lie, but not quite truth. 'Grandpa. Don't.'

'Well,' he said, and then chewed his bottom lip. 'I wanted to barbecue some fish Matt left me. A great filet of Kingfish fresh caught today.'

'And?' She cast him a sidelong glance. *There is no escaping that fish! She was not in the mood for eating fish after having the smell in her nostrils all day.*

'I heard from Jake.'

Her head swung around. 'What did he say?'

'Without going into too much detail, I don't want you alone with Drew Penderton. And maybe you should be careful about walking alone while he's in the neighborhood.'

She blinked. 'What did he do to Elena?'

Gregor stood up and stretched. He avoided looking her in the eye. 'He abducted her and threatened to rape her. The only thing that stopped him was the familial curse.'

A surge of fear swept through her, like a jolt of electricity. 'Oh ... that's no good.' She sat down heavily on the sofa, her legs not quite steady.

She thought about that date and his casual threat that he could rape her. He must have meant it. She hadn't mentioned the threat to Gregor explicitly, just that the word had been a topic of conversation. Maybe she should have. But nothing had come of it at the time. The incident walking home had tasted of Drew but was it him? If it had been, why would he try to threaten her? Drew had kept his distance, and his threat had been rather academic as he'd not tried to assault her sexually. Was it because he was getting good sex that she was safe?

What a pig he was. At first she had suspected there was something not right with him, but the evidence was building that he was a totally bad seed.

Her desire to tell Gregor about the incident was strong. Her grandfather had kept her pretty sheltered from dark magic, but she knew enough to recognize it—knew enough to be afraid.

'You're jumpy. What's the matter?'

She moved her body to face him and swallowed guiltily. She couldn't lie about this. An occurrence of dark magic was too important to keep to herself. 'I don't know exactly. Just something put me on alert.'

'Go on,' he said in a quiet voice.

'Nothing. That was it. I was walking home on the street, next to the park. Suddenly, I was alone, surrounded by nothing. Nothing could get in and nothing could get out.'

Gregor's eyes widened. 'You're sure?'

She waved a mosquito out of her face. 'Absolutely. I was able get out of it … eventually.'

Gregor's brows knitted together. 'That doesn't sound like a naturally occurring phenomenon. Drew?'

She had to answer truthfully. 'I thought it might be. There was a certain feel to the magic. What I experienced was new to me though. Only my eyes worked. My own fear mounted. I couldn't hail you … I was scared to my soul. My heart is still beating double-time.'

'A cloak that large?'

'Is that what you call it?' She shrugged, pretending not to be too upset. 'Maybe I was hysterical and it never happened like I imagined.'

'Maybe … Still, I want you to be careful.' He patted his middle. 'Come on. I'm hungry.'

Without reading him, she couldn't be sure, but she suspected a false calm.

'What do you mean be careful?' she asked as she followed Gregor into the kitchen.

He thrust a fishy-smelling bundle of paper at her. 'Don't burn my fish. And don't be on your own with Drew.' He tapped the tip of her nose.

Dodging away she wouldn't take the bundle. 'I'm not cooking your fish.' When he stopped trying to thrust it at her, she said, 'I scaled and cleaned it already when Matt caught it. I've done my bit.' She turned away.

'Nea?' He said with mock indignation.

Pausing, she shot him a grin over her shoulder. 'I'll make salad though.'

She opened the fridge and peered inside. 'What will it be? Potato, coleslaw or green salad?'

He went out to the barbecue and engaged the gas, then poked his head in the window. 'Why not do that nice pasta salad you made last weekend? The one with eggs and avocado.'

'Sure. I'll just clean up.'

Later, as they sat down to eat, she could tell something was bothering him, and it wasn't just that he'd asked her to date a potential rapist. 'What is it? Come on, Grandpa, spill.'

His eyes kindled. 'I've told you before, don't call me that.'

'Well, if you glower at your plate any longer it will transform into a Frisbee.'

He chuckled. 'Sorry. I was thinking about your experience with Penderton.'

'Well don't. It's done and dusted.'

He broke off the corner of a bread roll. 'I can't help it. I'm the head of this coven and I can't read him. I don't like not knowing the potential extent of his threats.'

She shook her head. 'I hear what you're saying. He has very strong barriers. So it goes without saying that he's deliberately hiding things, rather than being shy about his abilities.'

His eyelids quivered. 'Just be extra careful. Okay? I have a council meeting tonight, here. Will you be able to amuse yourself? I feel bad leaving you to your own devices after your fright. Maybe I should postpone the meeting.'

'Grandpa ... Gregor ... I'm fine.' She held out her hand. 'See? No tremors.'

'Stop patronizing me and have some respect. I'm the senior warlock around here and if you give me any more lip, I'm turning you into a frog.'

She made a frog sound and leapt away before he flicked her butt with a tea towel. When they stopped laughing, after trying to get at each other around the table, he stopped trying to swat her. 'I'm serious. Will you be all right, love?'

'Sure. I am over it. I might do a bit of navel gazing.'

His gaze went to the balcony. 'Not outside?'

She suppressed a groan. 'No, in my room. I have some serious thinking to do. You know: life, the universe … everything!'

He nodded. 'Well then. Be off with you before I find forty-two reasons to make you weed the garden with your teeth.'

As she headed for the door, the dishes flew off the table and slotted themselves into the dishwasher. Her eyebrows lifted. Gregor usually left the cleaning up to her and that was trivial use of magic.

As if reading her mind, he said, 'The council members are bringing their own snacks. You don't need to do anything for them.'

She frowned. 'Sure. No problem. Are you going to bring this business of Drew up with them?'

His face went blank. 'Council business, Nea. I won't discuss it with you.'

Using her talent, she shot a wet tea towel at him, which hit the back of his head. Laughing uproariously, she raced up the stairs to her room, while he sent a myriad of epithets after her.

'You can be a pain when you want to be, Grandpa!' she called from the top of the stairs.

'Wait for it, young lady. I can do better!'

Walking into her room, her door hit her in the butt, courtesy of her grandpa, and then swung shut. Recovering her balance, she tested the handle, and it wasn't locked. She blew a raspberry at the door and heard the lock engage. Then she laughed out loud and threw herself on her bed, feeling overwhelmed with love for the old man. She'd probably pay for that bit of disrespect tomorrow with him hexing her cup of tea or something equally silly.

She sighed loudly and kicked off her shoes. There was a problem, something bothering the old man, and she had no idea what it was. She hoped the rest of the council was aware of it. He could keep things from them and that wasn't good, not if it was serious.

He was good at getting her to talk about things she'd rather not discuss. Unfortunately, he was resistant to her attempts to get him to open up. How was she going to find out what the issue was? He was wily, and he'd pick up on any attempts she made to weasel it out of him.

The front door chimed. A council member had arrived. She let her talent sense who it was. It was Hilda, Gregor's second-in-charge. She always came early. Another chime and Wallace arrived with his wife, Elvie. Humphrey was parking his car, and he'd brought Siv with him.

She withdrew her witchsense. There was no point in eavesdropping. Gregor would shield the meeting and she'd not even dare try to peek in case he caught her at it. That would take things a bit beyond fun and games.

CHAPTER FOUR

Nea started from sleep, overheated, agitated. She tried to order her thoughts and recall what had woken her. A dream? The details of it were scattered. It had been erotic, weird, even, but there had been no narrative, and there was no sense to be made of it.

Her talent swept the house, passing over her grandfather asleep in his bed. The councillors had long gone. No magic was at work in the building. Her talent swept beyond the walls and brushed up against the wards. They were intact. She was safe. There was no external source to be found for her sudden waking.

Her gaze shifted to her clock. It was two a.m. She lay there and panted, sweat gathering in the small of her back. She kicked off the sheet and spread her legs to let the air cool her down.

Vestiges of the dream clung to her. The curtains billowed, letting in a cool breeze. Peeling off her T-shirt, she lay in her underpants. Her nipples puckered in the night air, but she knew they'd been that way earlier in her dream, aching and throbbing as if being suckled hard. She remembered the responding throb in her clitoris. Whatever she had dreamed had turned her on.

As her heart slowed, her eyelids drooped again. She should probably stroke herself, ease her tension so she could fall back to sleep, but she was too tired.

Sleep had almost captured her when the soft stroke of breath on her thigh made her eyes snap open. With her heart thumping loudly in her ears, she jerked up onto her elbows, her body a ramp as she sent her senses into every corner of the room.

'Who's there?'

There was no response. She lay still, waiting for some tell-tale sign that she wasn't alone, but none came. Darkness surrounded her, and there was no living thing but her in the room. No heartbeat, no breathing, and no movement. It must have been her imagination. She had no idea she was so deprived sexually that her dreams would appear so real or make her horny.

Her state of arousal sunk into the fabric of her. Thoughts of intruders were replaced with those of need. She groaned and rolled on her side. It had been so long since she'd been intimate with anyone, tears welled in her eyes. Her hand slid into her underpants and her labia were swollen. She was aroused. A touch of her finger, and pleasure zinged up her spine. Why couldn't she remember the dream that had so obviously turned her on?

Her finger slid into her folds and she was wet, wetter than she could remember. What had got her so hot? She wished she knew because she'd bottle it.

A few strokes of her clitoris and she was surrendering to a bone-shuddering orgasm, crying out with it. *Goddess, I hope Gregor didn't hear that.* She rolled her eyes up. He probably did. *Blast.*

She flung herself over onto her back, listening to

the soft lap of the lake down against the beach. Instead of feeling tired after her orgasm, she was alert. She stripped off her underwear and strode naked to the window. Hiding her breasts with the curtain, she peered down to the shore. There by the pier was a shadow. It looked like a man. A familiar man. She squinted at the outline. It looked like that guy she'd met earlier ... Earl?

She watched, fascinated. Maybe he lived close by.

For a moment, she thought their gazes locked, but when she blinked he was gone. She stuck her head out the window and swept her gaze along the shore and the backyard. There was no one.

The memory of Earl's face flashed into her mind. There was something odd about him, yet he was attractive and oozed 'easy-going'. She liked him—well, what she'd seen of him so far. She shook her head, glad she hadn't read him and spoiled the fantasy.

Back in bed, she lay there staring at the ceiling. Thoughts of Drew lingered, and the moment when she'd touched something in the ruin, a presence, a hunger. That place had frightened her—that was why she was thinking of it now. She tried a calming mantra but when that didn't help, she pulled on her singlet and groped for fresh underwear. She wasn't sleepy anymore but it was too early to get up. She didn't want her grandfather asking questions, which he would do if she started pottering around the kitchen, making tea or toast. The downside to living with someone.

Resigned, she put on her light and picked up a book from the floor beside her bed. It was a handbook of battle magic, a book for beginners, written by Declan Mallory. She'd met him briefly at Jake and Elena's joining celebrations, and again when she'd babysat on her last trip to Sydney. He was a good, solid warlock. He was a good, solid man too, well-built and good-looking. Too bad there weren't more where he came from.

She glanced at the book. It couldn't hurt to learn defense, and maybe it would help her decide what she wanted from life, whether to embrace her talent or forget about it in pursuit of love and children. The philosophy was familiar and the first few exercises seemed easy. About ten pages into the battlemage book, her eyelids drooped. She lay back down against her pillows, sprawled with her legs apart on the bed, and promptly fell asleep. Vaguely, she was conscious of the book falling to the carpet but it didn't rouse her, and she sank deeper into sleep.

In the morning when she went downstairs, Gregor was nowhere to be found. She was about to hail him when she found a note. He was out on council business and he wanted her to stay indoors. She blinked a few times, then sniffed when she put the note back on the kitchen counter. *So I can't go out now. That's just insane.* She looked through the window. It was a lovely day. No way was she staying inside. A walk around the lake was what she needed.

The coffee machine hissed as she teased her milk into froth. Then, topping off a large mug, she searched the bench-top for the chocolate but changed her mind and sprinkled cinnamon on instead. Waving the mug under her nose, she inhaled and closed her eyes. That had to be heaven—the smell of coffee in the morning.

Out on the back veranda, she sat on a lounger and sipped her coffee while watching the lake. It was a bit overcast so the water was a pale gray and the surface was so smooth it was like glass. As she reclined there, taking sip after sip, she decided she was definitely heading out, no matter what Gregor had decreed.

The walk around the lake was lovely—scudding clouds, toddlers laughing at the water's edge while their mothers gossiped on the shore. Near the park, she saw someone familiar leaning on the post. It was Earl. He had a smile on his face and waved to her. She smiled back in response.

'Hello,' she said as she walked up, keeping her reading skills in check, even though now she was dying to check him out.

'Hi. Nice day for a walk.'

'Yes. It is.' She shaded her eyes as she looked at him.

'Are you in a hurry?'

She screwed up her nose. 'God no. Just killing time and enjoying the lake.'

He stepped aside so she could see the bench. 'Would you like to sit here a bit and talk?'

She made a quick assessment and thought why not. 'Sure, I could do that. Wouldn't you like to walk with me?'

His face clouded. 'I can't … sore knee.'

The bench was handy so they took a seat. He grinned, his eyes showing a sparkle of light. 'So tell me. How long have you lived here?' he asked her.

She sat back, enjoying the sun's warmth. 'All my life.'

He nodded and relaxed against the bench. 'In your blood then. The lake is full of energy, isn't it?'

She nodded and lowered her eyelids. There didn't seem to be any talent emanating from him so she didn't take him for folk. Perhaps he was a new-ager type who adopted pagan ways, with his talk of the lake and energy.

She sent her gaze out over the water. 'Yes, I guess so. It harnesses energy from the sea.'

'And the moon,' he said, his voice rich.

She smiled. 'And the sun.'

Their gazes met and then he looked back out across the gentle waves. 'I used to paddle around in my canoe on the lake when I was young. I'd spend hours out there. My parents came here from France, and the culture shock hit them in a big way. Me? I just loved being on the water.'

'And you've just come back here?'

His smile fell away and his eyes darkened as they met hers. 'Yes.'

That was too much temptation. She reached out with her talent and tried to lightly read him. She got nothing. No thoughts—just a sense of calm. Her head jerked suddenly, her witchsense tingling.

'What is it?' he asked her.

'Nothing,' she responded quickly to cover herself. Her gaze flicked over his clothing. He was wearing the same clothes as yesterday, but there was no smell of coffee or cigarettes, just the briny scent of the lake.

'So do you work around here?' she asked, trying to pry but pretending not to.

'Not at the moment. I'm between jobs. You?'

'Ah, you saw me yesterday. I work a couple of days a week on the boat.'

He nodded. 'That must be nice.' He looked away to the lake and then back at her, a smile lifting the corners of his mouth. 'I like you.'

She blinked, not quite believing what she had heard. 'I'm sorry?'

He locked gazes with her. His voice lowered. 'I like you a lot.' His lips were full and kissable. She tried not to think about that, or the tanned hands that rested on his knees. He seemed so laid-back that she was almost tempted to lean against his chest and rest there.

'Thanks, but you hardly know me.'

'That's not true. Sometimes you meet someone and you know them.'

She nodded. 'Yes, that can happen but—'

'—not to you.'

She chuckled. 'Okay. You got me. That was what I was thinking.'

His forehead furrowed lightly. 'I understand the loneliness you feel. I feel it too. When you smile, it's like the rays of the sun are born in me and I fill up with light.'

She sucked in a breath. He sounded so sincere, and those words hooked into her heart. No one had expressed a feeling like that, not about her or to her. 'I don't know what to say except thank you for saying so.'

'You don't need to thank me. You are tied to this place like I am. You love it here and I understand that. In my innocent youth I loved it too. Now, I can see that same bond in you and I feel my own heart warming to the place all over again.'

She squirmed inwardly. This conversation was unnerving her. It was like he spoke to her heart, by-passing her brain. It was like he could read her, but that wasn't possible. He wasn't one of the folk. He didn't have the vibe—just a wall of calm emanating from him.

'I do love this place.' She shrugged, trying not to let on how close he came to speaking to her heart. There was a bond forming there and that was strange. They hadn't touched, not even to shake hands, yet they had a connection.

He let out a soft sigh. 'Yes, me too. It sustains me.'

She gazed into his eyes. 'I know what you mean.'

'Bethanea, goddess of the lake,' he whispered, and the hair on her neck prickled.

She wasn't sure how long they gazed at each other

before she shook herself and stood up. 'Look, I'd better head back home now.'

His smile dropped. 'Really? Already?'

She hated how hurt he looked, but she was rattled and touched and drowning in uncertainty and need. 'Maybe I'll bump into you again.'

Backing away, she gave him a smile.

He lowered his eyes, his expression suddenly dejected. 'Sure. Have a good walk back.'

She was grateful he didn't offer to accompany her, but kind of sad she didn't invite him.

After taking a few steps, she turned and waved. The bench was empty. The mothers chatting by the shore stopped and gaped at her, and then looked to where she waved. Turning away, she started walking, thinking them odd and rude, because they started talking and then laughing as she passed them by.

Earl watched Nea walk away and sighed. It was like watching the sun set and feeling the dew fall on bare skin. He was alone and at a loss as to how to connect with her. He knew he was drawn to her because she had caressed his essence and woken him back to life. He had tasted the very heart of her, and it was now part of him. The essential elements of her had meshed with his—an irresistible pull. For her sake he had found strength and had ventured out into the world, back to the beauty of the lake and the warmth of the sun to be with her, because of her. Danger swirled around her, and his protective feelings came to the fore. Yet, despite the altruistic impetus to his being there, other more selfish feelings had taken over. Now he'd seen that smile, touched that light essence of hers, he was lost.

What a contrast to his earlier choice. That had been a big mistake. Now he knew in his bones what was right and good for him. That was Nea. She was his 'one', but he was so unworthy. He wasn't truly alive—only the semblance of life gave him form. She deserved better than him, but still he wanted and desired her. There was no hope for them, but also all the hope in the world if they could only grasp it. She had touched him and roused him from that dark place. If she had achieved that much, then there was the chance for more.

He let the conjuring of himself fade, the substance of his phantom flesh dissipating. No point in using up his precious store of energy maintaining a form when she wasn't there. It was only for her that he'd bothered. It had been the only way to interact with her without scaring the bejesus out of her.

As he hovered there, wondering where to go next, he tasted regret. His decisions had been bad; they had cost him dearly. But he was still on this Earth so that must have meant something. There was a path to redemption somewhere. There had to be.

Within the hour, Nea was back home and out on the patio on a lounger. A bit of sun had broken through the clouds and she wanted to work on her tan. It was an impossible task as she was stubbornly pale. Luckily, with her talent she wasn't likely to get sun damage. Except for her freckles. She laughed to herself and rolled up her T-shirt to expose her belly and lay back with a sigh.

Her thoughts turned to Earl. She liked him, but she couldn't pinpoint what caused her disquiet. There was something odd about that light read of him. She detected a wall of calm but not much else. Yet she found him physically attractive, his eyes, his lips, and even the sound of his voice. And how he spoke to her in that honest way that connected directly to her heart. He was open without being fully readable. Not like unreadable Drew who gave nothing away, even in his expression.

She decided if she bumped into him again and he asked her on a date, she'd say yes. And if he didn't ask, maybe she would ask him out for a coffee. With a smile, she realized that maybe her man drought was broken. If Earl had been a warlock, she'd be a lost woman already.

Picking up her book, she tried to read, but the words meant nothing because she kept playing back that scene in the park with Earl, her heart skipping a beat when she remembered those words about loneliness and the lake. The wind picked up, smacking small waves against the shore, and a speedboat bounced across the surface, the burr of its engine echoing across the water. With the pages of her book open, she sighed as she drifted off to sleep.

She wasn't sure how long it was before a tingle against the house ward sent her lurching from the lounger.

With her heart thumping, she sent a hail to Gregor. *Is that you?*

Then she cursed herself. The ward would not tingle for him. He'd created it. It wasn't breached. Why was she so jumpy? She stepped back inside the house and crept to the front windows, looking out through the curtains to see who was there. The front yard was empty. No car. She stepped closer and looked sideways, but there was no one at the front door. The ward tingled again. What the hell was going on? This had never happened before.

She turned and stared at the stairwell. She'd go downstairs and check on the little bedsit there. Gregor should have answered her hail. She chewed her lip; something was definitely wrong.

Slowly, she took the stairs one by one, her gaze checking on the floor around her and then, as she got low enough, she could see the apartment. The door was closed. Nothing seemed to be touched. She walked into the bedroom and then went to look out the sliding door that provided access to the pier. A scan of the bushes to the left revealed nothing un-usual, but to the right she noticed a camellia shrub moving against the wind, pink petals floating to the ground.

Her heart thumped. Again, the ward tingled.

Sliding the door quietly open, she slipped out, ro-tating her head to keep everything in sight. She stepped around the bush and let out a cry.

'Grandpa!'

Gregor was sprawled in the dirt, blood leaking from a gash in his forehead, and his clothes had singe marks. She inhaled the scent of magic around him. Gregor Royston had been in a magical fight and he'd come off the worse.

He groaned, and she threw herself down next to him. 'Is it bad? Should I send for Hilda?'

'No,' he said in a tight voice. 'Just help me inside. I'll be better soon.'

'You think?'

She squatted down so that he could use her as leverage to get up. Once she had him in a sitting po-sition, the deal got a bit harder. 'Shouldn't I call someone to help? One of the councillors maybe?'

He shook his head. 'No. I'm fine.' He tried to get up and rocked back on his rear end. 'You'll have to give me your hand.'

She got to her feet and tugged until Gregor had enough momentum to stand, then she placed herself under his arm and supported him into the house. She had no idea how she was going to get him up the stairs. 'Maybe you should lie down here and I'll go get the first-aid kit.'

'No, no. Take me to my room to lick my wounds.'

'If you say so.'

It took quite a while to work their way up the stairs. Each step was laboriously conquered. Luckily, his bedroom was on the main level, whereas her room was upstairs. With a groan, he flopped down on the bed, and she went scurrying for some hot water, a cloth and some bandages.

'Don't fuss. I can seal up the cuts later.'

Annoyed at her efforts being so casually dismissed, she said archly, 'How come you can't heal them now?'

'I'm depleted. I'm in shock—not quite there. Need time.'

Her eyebrows arrowed together. 'Can you tell me what happened?'

'Later. I will.'

She marched off to get her medical supplies. She didn't care what a kick-up he made, she was treating his injuries whether he liked it or not.

When she made it back to the room, Gregor was snoring. Gently, she wiped the blood on his forehead and examined the wound. It looked superficial, but she was worried anyway. In all her life, she'd never known him to be defeated. He'd always been this strong magical figure, able to do things she could never dream of. Seeing him like this made her worry, made her feel vulnerable.

What could possibly have happened to him? *It has*

to be Drew. She was itching for Gregor to tell her about it.

Once she had him cleaned up, she hailed one of the council members, the second-in-command, Hilda.

The phone rang instantly, and Hilda was on the other end. 'You found him in the garden, injured?' Hilda sounded surprised and perturbed.

'Yes. Can you tell me what's going on?'

'Even if I knew, I couldn't tell you, aye. It's up to Gregor to let you in on it.'

'Did you want to come over and check on him?'

'No. He sounds fine to me with you looking after him, but do let me know if he doesn't pick up after a sleep. Make him lay low for a few days until his energy builds up again. Give him a hearty meal. There you go. That's it. One of your smashing cook-ups ought to do it.'

'Thanks.' Nea glared at the phone and hung up. Things were not normally so cloak-and-dagger in their coven.

She hesitated by the phone, wondering if she should call Jake or her dad and let them know. Her dad, Riley, was up on the Great Barrier Reef, enjoying a holiday with his current girlfriend. No point in spoiling it for them. Jake would likely front up, and then there would be consequences. She turned away from the phone, deciding that Gregor would hate having a fuss made, and probably wouldn't like the fact he'd come off badly in an altercation known.

She checked on her grandfather, who was still sleeping, and then tried to interest herself in a half-finished novel sitting on a side table. When that didn't stick, she went to the computer and surfed the net, having a chuckle over some sites that purported to be teaching spells and magical ceremonies.

After making herself some supper, she checked on her grandfather again, and he appeared to be sleeping normally. She placed a jug of water by his bed, and some fruit in case he woke up hungry during the night.

Then she went to get ready for bed. The shower was hot and the water pressure was good. She was tempted to stay in there but knew she had to get out sometime. Standing there naked, she gazed longingly at her bed. It looked so inviting. Not much had been achieved that day, but she was tired.

She checked the windows, stopping to cast a glance to where she'd seen the man's shadow the night before. There was nothing on the pier, and there was nobody walking along the shore taking in the night air. She had to admit to being a bit disappointed.

Next, she reset the house wards. Then she remembered she'd left the downstairs sliding door open as she'd been caught up in finding Gregor and treating his injuries.

With a sigh, she wrapped herself in a robe and went below. Gregor's snoring could be heard in the corridor as she passed through to take the stairs. He was really spent. He'd better tell her what was going on or she was going to be hopping mad, council business or not.

The sliding door was open, the night breeze kicking up the curtain. Hurrying over, she went to shut it and paused. The bushes rustled more vigorously than the wind could account for. She squinted into the dark. Goosebumps rose on the skin of her arms. She ranged out with her senses. There was a ward, she shouldn't have to worry about intruders, and yet there was something there, something or someone watching her.

Pulling herself inside, she slid the door shut and locked it. Someone was playing a sick game and she wasn't going to join in.

Stamping her way up the stairs, she threw open her door and tore off her robe. Using her talent, she flung the covers off and slid onto the bed, then she flicked the lights off with a blink and found herself stewing in the darkness. It wasn't really the right mindset for going to sleep, but she rolled over and shut her eyes anyway.

Sometime in the night, the window rattled. In a daze, she got up to close it, and found it already shut. Her eyes caught some movement. There was nothing outside, yet there was a brush of something down her bare back. Her spine arched, her breath sucked in, and then she whirled around. 'Who is it?'

She flicked the light switch with her power, but it didn't come on. A sensation brushed against the skin of her shoulder, like a cool breath. Again, she whirled around, but could see nothing. 'Whoever you are this isn't funny.'

A vibration reached her, soothing her nerves. It meant no harm, whatever it was. That was the message she got. It definitely wasn't Drew Penderton or a conjuring of his.

She tried for the lights again and still nothing.

'I don't like this. Go away.'

The presence withdrew, but she wasn't alone. Air moved around her. Whatever it was it had some kind of form. Her mind yelled that it was a ghost, a friendly one, but her reading suggested something more tangible. She didn't know, and as it stayed away from her for the moment she could relax. Tentatively, she sent a hail to Gregor, just a little one to see if he was conscious, but there was nothing. He was out of it. She was on her own.

Her nipples contracted to hard points. She gasped as she felt a mouth close over one, but it wasn't a mouth. It wasn't warm and wet, yet there was pressure.

She backed away, not sure who or what she was backing away from. The thought crossed her mind that this was a figment of her frustrated imagination. A very interesting figment, certainly. Hadn't she been wishing for intimacy, for sex? Her breathing reverberated in the room, seeming loud to her panicked ears.

That vibration again, signaling the presence was there, was close. The vibration soothed her fears. It meant no harm; it liked her, and wanted to be close to her. It wasn't quite a reading, but it was something else.

In the darkness, she couldn't work out where she was walking, but she was backing up. The backs of her knees hit the mattress and she collapsed on the bed.

Staring at the darkness, she wondered how she was going to explain this and hoped that she never had to. Perhaps it had been a dream. Then, a phantom mouth glanced against her mons and a ghostly tongue lapped against her labia.

Goddess! A shudder ran up her spine. Her body responded to her phantom lover.

That mouth pressed there again, harder.

'Stop. Please.' She eased up on her elbows, panting heavily. The presence withdrew from her. For that she was grateful, because it allowed her time to think, to assess and to push away the raw need that had been nagging at her for weeks now—the need to be touched and to be loved and to be held. Now this thing, this presence, tempted her at her weakest point.

'Who are you? Please tell me.'

She got a sense of agreement, then the scene around her changed. She wasn't in her bedroom; she was on the lakeshore and it was the afternoon. Yellow sun glinted off the water. She had a dress on, an old-fashioned thing. *What?*

A man walked towards her, dark hair curling around his forehead, slightly long on his collar. It was Earl, the man she'd been meeting the last two days.

She watched him approach, thinking his large eyes were dark brown until he stepped up close. Then in the light she saw they were hazel, green, yellow and brown mixed together. His mouth was full and dark red, entirely kissable. His nose gently curved, giving him a regal air. Was this a fantasy?

She looked around. Not fantasy. Not her fantasy, at least. It wasn't real. She was in her bedroom. This was a conjuring. With her talent, she tested the edges of it. It was a good conjuring. It had substance. Whoever had made it was gifted and strong.

'You're right,' he said as he stood in front of her. 'It's a conjuring. I made it so we could talk.'

'Talk? What are you, Earl?' She picked up those calming vibrations she'd sensed in her room.

'I'm me.'

'And that is …?'

'I wanted to thank you.'

She chewed her lip. 'Thank me?'

'Yes,' he said, and he smiled, and it transformed his face into charm itself. He didn't take his eyes off her. 'You're very beautiful. A beautiful spirit with a sweet face. I knew it the moment we met.'

She backed up a step. 'Earl. We've only just met, briefly.'

Her gaze took in his form—broad shoulders, the firm arms. He was wearing a shirt and trousers. If she'd been out with friends for a drink and had come across him, she'd be fanning herself.

'Yes. But before that. Don't you remember? You woke me.'

She closed her eyes, wanting to block the image of him out. It was messing with her head. 'You're that thing I touched in the ruin. In that place of dread and death. A ghost?'

'I'm not a ghost. Not entirely.' There was a lift to his lips, an almost-smile that reached in and hooked her. Bedroom eyes, a kiss-me mouth, and a fuck-me-all-night body. This had to be her own imagination.

That hint of a smile blossomed. He lifted a hand and moved some hair off her face. 'This is what I used to look like.'

She didn't react, didn't object. It seemed such a natural thing for him to do. 'What are you then?'

'I'm not dead. Perhaps I should be. I was a war-lock; now I'm less than I was.'

She spread her hands, indicating her surround-ings. 'This isn't real. You're not real.'

'I am real but … I'm not flesh. Not anymore.' He smiled at her, the light in his eyes telling her he liked what he saw.

Great. I found a warlock but he's not flesh, not a ghost, and not quite alive. Just my luck. The undead man of my dreams.

'But you like me all the same.'

'How did you …?'

His arms went around her. He'd heard her thoughts. That wasn't fair. 'Let me go.'

He stepped away. 'I'm sorry. I didn't mean to im-pose. I could feel your want from outside. We have a …' He shrugged and then grinned. 'A connection.'

Had he really heard all her thoughts? *Goddess!* She coughed and looked down at her feet. They were bare, which was at odds with the dress. As she looked on, red sandals formed.

'That's a neat trick.'

His dark eyebrows drew together. 'I thought you wanted intimacy.'

She blinked at him. 'I do, but I … er … well … part of that is getting to know you.'

He looked up and the sky was suddenly night, and they stood under a lamp by the lake's edge. 'That's why I conjured this, so we could get to know each other so you would feel safe. I won't hurt you.'

'I appreciate that, but I was looking for a more conventional relationship. Like with a living, breathing warlock with the possibility of a home, family …'

His eyes widened fractionally. 'I'm sorry. This is the best I can do for now.'

A wave of hurt washed over her and she was sorry for her words. Then she could read him in a rush—the pain, the suffering swamped her and she had to back pedal, had to withdraw. Had to stop reading him.

'I'm sorry,' he said, his voice warm and vibrant. 'I didn't mean for you to see. I forgot for a moment you're a reader.'

She struggled for speech, she was so over-whelmed.

He backed away from her. 'I'll leave you alone.'

The image that he'd constructed began to curl at the edges as if burnt by flame. 'Wait,' she said, gasping. She brought her own emotions under control. 'I don't want you to go yet. Talk to me some more.'

His suffering called to her. It was a pain beyond her imagining. It hooked her empathy and told her there was more there: depth and love and intel-ligence.

The image stabilized. He was back in front of her, his dark gaze traveling over her skin, eating her up. 'You're a goddess, not only of this lake, but of my heart.'

Her eyelids fluttered. 'Earl,' she began.

'Part of you is in me. When you touched me with your essence you left part of yourself there. I feel as if I know you, as if I'm drawn to join with you so what you left behind can be whole again.'

'I didn't realize ...'

He touched her lips with a ghostly finger. 'Shh ... it's all right.' He studied her face. 'I love the shape of your eyes and the cute freckles on your nose.' He kissed the tip of it softly. The touch was like electricity.

'Earl ... I ...' She narrowed her gaze, trying to order her thoughts. All she had to do was reach out to him. He was open to her.

The need in him called to her heart. Softly, he caressed her head, combing his fingers through her hair, his thumb brushing gently on her jaw. She closed her eyes, imagining him kissing her, nuzzling her everywhere.

Her eyes snapped open. She looked down and she was naked. She gaped. 'What the ...?'

He had read her thoughts, responded to her need.

His hand around her waist drew her forward. 'You are naked in your bedroom. I've seen your gorgeous body. It's been tempting me all this time.'

'Oh, it's a bit confronting, you know. I haven't seen a conjuring like this since I was little. Gregor conjured a circus for the coven.'

'Gregor?'

'My grandfather, Gregor Royston.'

He frowned slightly and smoothed his hand down her head. 'Again I apologize.'

She smiled at his contriteness. 'It's fine, really …' She wanted to say more but was caught by the glow in his eyes and the way it stirred her.

'I know how to pleasure you.'

'You do?'

'Yes, if you'll let me.'

His head lowered and some fit of abandon made her lift her mouth to his. And the kiss, she dived into it. Like a pool of warm water, it surrounded her. His mouth demanded and she submitted, then the tide turned and she took the lead, and he let her sink into him. On and on the kiss went. She forgot to breathe until at last, like a wave leaving seaweed on the shore, she landed, clinging to him, her breath coming in big gulps.

Wow. That was some kiss.

Through the kiss she could taste his loneliness, years and years of it, and it tapped into her own. The ache for intimacy, the need to be desired, the joining of spirit and flesh. *I'm so there.*

They continued kissing, wrapped in each other's arms, and talking quietly. She put her head against Earl's chest, so comfortable in his embrace that she knew she belonged there.

'So, Bethanea Royston, may I make love to you?' His dark eyes were soft embers.

Goddess yes!

I cannot mate with you fully, but I can give you fulfillment.

Oh please …

And the conjuring vanished and she was back in her room, naked on her bed, her legs hanging over the edge where she'd landed previously. A moment of dislocation followed as she adjusted to the change of scene. Earl's conjuring had been absorbing and realistic.

Awakened to his presence when his head dipped her to breasts, she groaned. He said he could not penetrate her, but he was able to bring pressure to bear so his touch seemed real. When his lips closed on her nipple, it was like a real mouth. Closing her eyes, she gloried in the tug and pull as he teased her flesh. He drew down on her nipple, sucking it into his throat. The sensation was glorious. Arching her back, she groaned as her breasts ached and stung, bringing her to the brink of pleasure and pain.

Deep within her abdomen a burning tingle grew, making her vulva moisten and then throb. The sensation of drawing down as he drank from her was seriously turning her on. Desire uncoiled within her, sending her skin tingling, snaking along her body so that she whimpered. He pressed her hands against the bed, and that restraint upped her arousal further.

His hands massaged her breasts, squeezing the flesh so more imaginary milk would flow. The more he suckled, the greater the pressure, and she writhed and moaned, crying out when caught between pain and arousal. Still, he did not let up. Never had her breasts been teased into so much pleasure.

The desire to stroke his head grew, but her hands were pinned. She could not touch him, nor rake her nails down his back, nor pull his hair nor caress his shoulders. She bit back a moan. The thought of being restrained unleashed her passion.

She thrust up her hips, demanding that he suckle her there. Her clitoris throbbed as she moved. She wanted to stroke herself, let the pleasure wash over her, but she couldn't move her hands. She thrust upward, demanding the stroke of mouth or tongue or finger or cock.

The pressure on her nipples released and she let out a long sigh. She was regretful that the excruciatingly erotic sensation had stopped, yet her nipples were free of pain and puckered in the night air. Then, light touches brushed against her labia, and possessed of an eager hunger, she opened her legs wider and thrust up, begging to be brought to climax. Her body stilled, waiting for the next teasing lick between her moist folds. It came long and lush, making her cry out. A firm pressure, not quite a tongue, not quite a mouth.

Her body shuddered, her breath caught, and sweat broke out on her lower back, under her arms and across her forehead. The anticipation made her tremble. What would he do next?

Then he latched on, sucking gently on the nub of her sex. It was excruciatingly delightful. Whimpers and moans came fast and hard. The desire to beg grew like fire in her belly. She clamped down on it. She couldn't, shouldn't beg.

Again, as he teased her flesh, it was like he drank from her, lapping at some invisible milk. His tongue grew firmer, his lips more demanding. Thrusting in and out, he fucked her with his mouth. Just that thought had her shouting. *Thank the Goddess Gregor is out cold.*

Her hips rose up and down in sync with his rhythm. Her cries were broken sounds, gasps when she came close and then lowering to guttural grunts when he eased off. She was being played, being driven to extremes, being explored, tested, ridden.

Fuck me, she wanted to say. *Fuck me hard.* But even with her phantom lover, the words were hard to say.

He brought her so close, she almost came, and then he stopped. Tears wet her face and then she sobbed like a bereft child. Why had he stopped? *Don't stop, please.*

Turn over.

She rolled over, her butt exposed to the night air, assisted into position by a ghost hand. She had to remember that he'd said he couldn't penetrate her. What was he doing? He had stopped, and she'd been so close to climax.

Then there was pressure there, parting her butt cheeks. His vibration changed; it thrilled rather than soothed. Then the tongue was back, putting pressure where she'd never experienced it before. It was alien. It was strange.

Her breath caught, uncertain. The pressure continued, bathing her like a firm tongue but not. It was amazing. He pleasured her, positioning her so that her hips were cocked at an angle, as if she were begging to be licked like that, as if she liked the pressure of his tongue as she opened to him as she never had to anyone before.

Her mind knew elation. He drew shudders from her body and cries from her lips. He was touching the core of her, wringing the pleasure from her. Her legs shook from the ecstasy and her hands clawed the sheets as she yelled with triumph when the orgasm shook her to the core. Then she collapsed onto the mattress as tiredness enveloped her. She couldn't speak, couldn't even think her thanks when an exhausted sleep swallowed her whole.

Earl stood on the pier, his essence tingling as it absorbed the energy that had bled from Nea like honey from honeycomb. The more he'd suckled, the more she'd given, filling him up, making him feel like he was going to explode. His substance was growing stronger and that delighted him. He longed for a real life, real flesh. And after a life of darkness and emptiness, he longed for real love, and finally understood that such a thing was possible.

Nea was delightful—so giving, so sensual, so willing to surrender to the moment. He'd pushed her beyond her norm. He was proud of that. He'd given her something no one else had. He wanted to give her so much more. Looking at the substance of his hand, he knew he could not.

He wasn't quite alive. Not flesh. Not the flesh she needed and wanted. At best, he could be the phantom that visited her in the night to pleasure and seduce her. If she took a mate, he'd have to watch, only sneaking in to pleasure her when her mate was absent from her bed. He frowned. If she was his he'd never be absent from her bed. He'd never let some phantom lover pleasure her.

Frustrated, he turned away. He had suffered for his crimes, paid a price, and he didn't want to continue to do so. Was being with Nea the ultimate punishment, showing him what he could have but was denied? All because of his mistake. All because of his weakness. All because of betrayal.

The strands of morning pierced the horizon. He had to take shelter. The ruin was the last place he wanted to go, but it was where he was safe. It was there he could hide himself in shadows and despair. It was there he could think of her and absorb the energy she'd so sweetly gifted him. He hated to leave her alone. Maybe soon he wouldn't have to.

Maybe he would fuck her for real one day and catch those cries of hers in his mouth, sharing them with no one, not even the night air. He frowned though, remembering how the energy had poured out of her into him. He was a vacuum, a suck-space that drew everything in, an instinctive hunger he couldn't control.

With a glance at her window, he shook with realization. He'd fed from her. He hadn't meant to. He'd only wanted to dally, to tease, to see how far he could take her but her energy had been so sweet, so juicy that once he'd suckled her teat and tasted her he hadn't been able to stop. He'd had to draw more of her in, suck her down into the fabric of himself. The way she'd responded had egged him on. Her moans, her whimpers, and her small sounds of ecstasy had made him dive in. How he wished he could brush real fingers across her skin, that his real mouth could lap her essence and that his real fingers could probe her.

Yet, he hoped he had not harmed her, for that was the last thing on his mind. She had smiled on him in a dark place. Her warm spirit had stirred him from slumber. He didn't wish to repay that kindness with injury. To injure her was to harm himself.

He was remorseful; he'd not meant to take it so far. Licking her anus had had him quivering with delight. Energy had poured out of her the more he'd opened her up. Leaving her on the verge of orgasm had backed up the energy inside her and it had been craving for a way out, for release.

Her surrender had been extraordinary. What would it be like to fuck her with a real flesh cock, to feel the slide of her against his skin, the squeeze of her muscles against his erection? How could it be any more extraordinary than what had transpired that night? But he knew it could and would be. There was so much promise in Nea. *Bethanea.*

A sense of longing demanded that he stay, and then his gaze slid to the east where the sun was making its mark. He was so full of Bethanea he was fit to burst. Taking time was necessary to adjust to this new level of energy. He'd leave her now, but he'd be back. To watch and guard and protect. She was his now.

Before he left, he detected something in the garden around the house, a sinister thread of threat, kept at bay by a ward. He sniffed the air, tasted it on his tongue. He'd have to stay close. There was danger here. He couldn't tell if it was a specific threat for Nea, but something was there, woven into the fabric of the air.

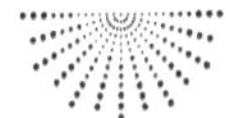

CHAPTER FIVE

The sunlight blinded her painfully when Nea awoke the next morning. Screwing her eyelids tight, it took her a few goes before she could open them. The brightness seemed to burn into her brain.

She was so tired, she could hardly move her head. She tried to prop herself up on her elbows but they wouldn't obey her commands. Turning her head towards her clock, she groaned. The clock read ten a.m. She blinked. It still read ten a.m. That wasn't possible. She never slept late.

On trying to roll over, she found that she couldn't. She was as weak as a tepid cup of chamomile tea. She tried again and managed to flop a leg over the side of the bed. That was all she could do. Allowing herself to roll onto her back, she stared at the ceiling wondering what the hell had happened.

With intense concentration, she managed to send a weak hail to Gregor, wondering if she should bother him at all in his condition, but then again, he might wonder where she was and what was wrong. She was normally up and about cleaning, tidying, cooking—whatever by now. Weakly, she groped for the sheets to hide her nakedness and after a few attempts, dragged the thin cotton material over herself.

Gregor took his time responding, and she wondered if she'd lost the ability to hail. *In bed, you?*

He came through loud and clear, and she let out a sigh of relief and blinked back a tear or two. *Me too. Sorry.*

You okay? She could almost see the furrows between his eyebrows as he frowned.

She resisted the urge to weep and feel sorry for herself. *Yes, I'm fine. Didn't sleep well so I'm laying in.*

Perhaps it was stupid to lie, but he sounded so out of form himself that she couldn't tell him that she was so weak she was frightened. She was ashamed, too, because she had a feeling that she was the cause of her own weakness, and she didn't really want to explore the how of it. It wasn't as if she would willingly confess to letting some undead warlock she'd accidentally awakened pleasure her sexually during the night.

Her cheeks burned when she recollected what had happened. Her muscles clenched at the thought of it. It had been the most amazing sex she'd had in her life. They'd done things she'd not even dreamt about. While she was weakened so that she felt near to death, there had been no malice involved. She was certain of that. The reading from him during the night had opened him up like a book to her—his desire, his sorrow and regret, and his honest feelings of love. He really did consider that in her he had found his match. She groaned at the ceiling. *Why did fate have to be so cruel?* There could be no future for them, but she'd do it again, even feeling as she did now.

❀

In the early evening, her grandfather laboriously climbed the stairs and came into her room. She hadn't moved from the bed. She'd need help to get to the toilet so she'd held on, hoping her strength would return, but it hadn't so far.

He groaned as he sat on the edge of her bed, his cheeks sagging with fatigue. He looked twenty years older than when she'd last seen him. 'Nea?'

'Yes,' she replied weakly.

'What is it?'

'I don't know,' she said faintly, her head lolling on the pillow.

Gregor reached out and touched her head. There was a tingle when his talent seeped into her. He pulled back suddenly. 'What have you done?'

She blinked at him. A tear leaked from her eye to dampen the pillow. 'I don't know.' A sob broke out of her; she was truly sorry for herself.

'Hush now. Don't cry. You are nearly empty of energy, barely a thread left.'

Her eyes widened and she thought *how*, but then her face heated. She knew the how.

'You really don't know?' He shook his head, raking his hand through his gray-blond hair.

'No.' Even her voice sounded weak. The tears fell more readily then as she realized the depth of her predicament. She didn't have enough energy to sob or wipe at her tears; they just sunk into her pillow.

'I'm wrecked myself. I've sent for Hilda. We need her help.'

'I need to use the bathroom.'

He stumbled about, looking for a bedpan. They had a few from when they had nursed her grandmother. She did her best not to be embarrassed as he assisted her.

'That's that,' he said, and collapsed on the edge of her bed. 'Hilda's on her way. I suggest you do whatever she says by way of healing. I don't want her complaining to me that you're being stubborn.'

After the door shut behind him, she closed her eyes, too fagged to even try for a cheeky comeback. Gregor was the king of stubborn and she was pretty sure Hilda knew that. The whole coven knew how cantankerous he became if he was impeded in any way.

If she was too weak to get out of bed, her grandfather was only marginally better off. He'd been sleeping for longer, but as she listened to his slow progress down the stairs, she knew they were both in very vulnerable positions.

If Earl hadn't intended to drain her, how had it happened? The detail of what he'd done to her was very precise in her memory. Her cheeks burned. How was she going to admit to that? She couldn't even lie and say it had been a dream. That would be wrong. It was a simulated sexual encounter, but not as simulated as she'd thought, given her energy deficit.

Her tears continued to flow. The memory of her interlude with Earl replayed like moments of real life. Just thinking of what that tongue had done to her and how she'd begged in her mind for more gave her a sinking feeling. It wasn't that she was a prude, but none of her sexual encounters had taken her so close to the edge. The encounter with Earl had thrown her off the deep end. She trembled at the thought of the blatant and abandoned way she had begged him. The resulting shattering ecstasy that had left her gasping had been the reward for opening herself up. It was hard to regret it, even now as she lay there, helpless.

The sound of Hilda arriving startled her. She lay there waiting while she heard the tell-tale signs of an argument. The older witch was winning. She could only hear weak, dull tones from her grandfather. Footsteps on the stairs and the wake of Hilda's power let her know to expect her.

The door flung open. Hilda wore black tights, with a longish tunic in a dull purple color, ending just above her knees. Her light brown Polynesian skin contrasted with her lovely white teeth. With her hands on her hips, she frowned as her gaze swept the room. 'You too, aye?' Hilda said in a no-nonsense tone, her talent like a swift breeze as it assessed her.

'I need to pee again.' She couldn't shrug so she looked pitiful instead. 'I need help, please.'

Hilda's brows drew together and then she located the bedpan, tut-tutting as she assisted. 'Now that your immediate needs are cared for, I have to have a closer look at what Gregor's done to himself. You, I can tell, aren't going anywhere.' Then she went over to the en-suite bathroom and filled a glass. 'Let me help you drink this, first.'

She drank as much of the water as she could and then sunk back onto the pillow.

'I'll be back. Best you rest for now, but by the look of you, I'd best fetch my potion-making material and cooking pot. You are probably worse than Gregor estimated. I'll fix you both up quickly. It's not a good time to be depleted.'

Nea smiled weakly and dropped off to sleep, intermittently hearing Hilda's voice, either chanting, arguing, or talking to herself.

Around midnight, Hilda came in, a steaming mug in her hands. 'Now, my girl, time for a serious chat. What have you done to yourself, hey? You're nearly drained. Gregor said so—a brilliant observation from a warlock who is nearly in the same boat—and I can see that for myself.'

She was too exhausted to reply. With a nod, the other witch brought over a chair and put the mug on the side table. 'Now I want to help you sit up because you are going to drink this potion, every last drop. You need this so you can be better by morning.'

She fluttered her eyelids, trying to rouse herself. There was not enough energy in her limbs to shuffle up the bed to a sitting position.

'That's the way of it, hey?' Hilda leaned over and assisted her into a more upright position, tugging pillows around her so she didn't flop over. The older witch sat on the bed next to her and kept her propped up while she supervised the drinking of the potion.

Nea opened her mouth, only too willing to be restored to herself, the sooner, the better. The day had been full of the agony of waiting and of feeling helpless. She couldn't remember feeling this way ever in her life.

As she sipped, she grimaced. *Why do potions taste like boiled slimy frogs and tadpole carcasses? Probably because they are essential ingredients.* If she hadn't felt so crap she would have laughed at her own joke. As it was, she was numb and totally unamused.

Her eyes flicked up to Hilda's face, noting that her skin was relatively unlined. Like the warlocks, some witches could slow their aging, and she suspected Hilda had this talent. Her hair was dark and naturally curly and her eyes were so brown they looked black. Her complexion was tanned but that was her Polynesian heritage, being a Maori from New Zealand.

Hilda made eye contact and smiled, bringing a shine to her face and displaying a pair of dimples that she had not noticed before. The older witch was attractive for her age. She was nicely built, not too thin and not too fat, and with nice curves. Her dress sense was about twenty years behind the times though, more like a hippy than a new-ager. No one could accuse of her of being trendy. Not like Elvira, Elena's adoptive mother. She had never seen a witch of that age look so fine. Elvira may not be able to slow her age as well as Gregor could, but she carried off the elegance so naturally one didn't notice.

Hilda fussed over her when the potion was done, talking to her in soft tones. 'Let me help you lie down now.' Not really having much energy to resist being placed gently against the pillow, she just blinked slowly and swallowed potion-laden spit. There was some cinnamon in there, elderberry, and something that tasted like grass but wasn't. The magic imbued into the potion made her tongue tingle and her throat burn, both welcome signals. She wasn't much of a potions study as she hadn't had much call for it. She'd focused on her strengths in a lackadaisical way —reading people and hanging about the house, looking after Gregor.

When she thought about it, she really hadn't tried very hard to do anything, and look where she was— flat out on her back, nearly drained. As she studied the ceiling, she realized that this was her moment. The time when she changed her life. Did something with it. Something worthwhile.

'I'm going to sit with you during the night, dear. You need more doses of the potion. Gregor is responding well. Another couple of doses and he'll be better than ever.' The older witch adjusted her chair and then tugged the sheets to Nea's chin, straightening out the wrinkles.

Hilda narrowed her gaze. Nea blushed as she was naked beneath the sheets. 'Perhaps you'd be more comfortable in a night gown?' Hilda went to the dresser, hesitated, and then opened the correct drawer.

'What about Grandpa? Won't you need to look after him?' She was embarrassed to take up so much of the older witch's time.

Hilda screwed up her face. 'I'll deal with Gregor, don't you worry.'

She kept her gaze on the other woman. There was something she wasn't saying. 'Will he be all right?'

Hilda waved a hand. 'No need to worry about him, hey? A warrior's heart and a warrior's mettle, that one.'

After she helped Nea into her nightie, Hilda sat back in her chair. 'You'll be able to get up tomorrow, I think. If you can manage it. The potion is working already. Gregor was right. He couldn't look after you in this state.'

During the night, Hilda woke her and made her sip more potion. The cure Hilda dispensed churned her innards, leaving her feverish and unsettled. When she was agitated, Hilda stroked her forehead and cooed to her as she massaged her scalp, sending her off to sleep again.

Come morning, she woke to see Hilda standing at the window gazing over the lake.

'What's it like today?' she asked, surprising herself that she had the energy to talk. Elbowing her way up the bed, she felt so much better.

Hilda turned and smiled. 'A sparkling sapphire today, with diamond lights on the water.' She sighed. 'I love this place so much.' She walked over to the bed and reached out to smooth Nea's hair. 'How are you feeling, hey?'

'A lot better. Thanks to you.'

Hilda waved her hand dismissively. 'None of that,' she said, her dark eyes assessing, looking beneath the surface. 'Yes, your energy levels have improved. You can get up. Gregor wants to talk to you.'

'He does?' Nea's face flushed. That was not a discussion she was looking forward to.

'Yes, I will tell him you'll be down in a jiffy.' Hilda paused at the door and grinned. 'You know, Nea. We're a coven, a family. You need to be open about what happened to you.'

Nea watched as the door snicked shut. A noise startled her, making her heart thump harder. Her eyes flicked around the room.

Earl's calm vibrations washed over her, then the room was conjured away. She lay on the grass by the lakeshore. Earl was there, stroking the ends of her hair.

'I'm so sorry,' he said. 'I had no idea that making love to you would drain you.'

'So it was that?'

'It must be. I'm full of energy, new energy and life. See ...?' He showed her his hand, moved it around and wiggled his fingers. 'I have more substance.'

She gazed at him, not quite able to smile.

'I couldn't come sooner. The witch was there the whole night tending you.'

A sigh escaped her and her eyes closed. They didn't touch but she was warmed by his presence.

Then she remembered her grandfather was waiting to talk to her. 'Gregor!' She blurted out. Her gaze met Earl's. 'I'm sorry, I have to go. I have some explaining to do.'

The conjuring faded and she was back in her room.

CHAPTER SIX

Nea made her way slowly downstairs and then walked into the kitchen. Gregor sat there with a steaming cup of potion in front of him and a militant glare in his eye. Hilda had two bright spots on her cheeks and her lips were firmly pressed together, as if she was biting back some vitriolic comeback.

'There you are. About time you were up and about. Hilda here has taken over the place.'

She groped for a chair and slid into it. Despite the potions, she wasn't her old self yet.

Hilda sniffed and started pouring a mug of potion. When the older woman handed it to her, she took it gratefully. 'Thank you.' She sipped it, hating the taste but knowing it was working to help her. Gregor slanted a snarling look at the other witch and the air crackled with tension. Had they been fighting?

She frowned at Gregor, who was almost strangling his mug.

'Hilda is helping us. Be nice.'

He harrumphed and took a large mouthful of brew. He didn't screw up his face as she did. He was made of sterner stuff. He lifted his head and directed his bright blue gaze at her. 'So what happened to you to get you into such a state?' he asked, his stare making her squirm. Her gaze flicked to Hilda. She supposed she couldn't exclude the woman. 'It wasn't Drew, was it?'

'No,' she replied immediately, aghast at the thought. 'It wasn't him.'

'Thank the Goddess for that then.' Gregor's shoulders slumped. The relief that Drew hadn't attacked her undermined his defenses and she was able to sneak a light read of him. He wasn't as healed as he made out.

Hilda let out a sigh. 'Drew Penderton? I know what you did, old man. You're a silly old warlock taking on Drew Penderton without back-up.'

Gregor's eyes flashed as he rounded on his second-in-command, but he had little of his normal power. In a defeated tone, he said, 'It's not your concern.'

'If it's not my concern why am I here looking after you, hey? Besides, I'm more concerned about Nea. I'd also like to know how she was drained nearly to death.'

Gregor's white eyebrows drew together. 'She's right, Nea. If it wasn't Drew, what happened to you?' His expression showed he expected no nonsense. 'Spill.'

She took another sip of her brew while she ordered her thoughts 'Recently, I met someone. Just a guy I thought, but then ...' She paused to swallow another sip of potion. 'Well, the night before last he was in my room. He can get through the wards, by the way. Ours at least. But he wasn't really in my room. Or maybe he was ...'

'What do you mean wasn't really in your room?' Gregor thundered at her.

'He's a warlock but he's … not … not alive.'

Gregor sat back. 'You're dating a ghost warlock?' His mouth opened and shut but no words came out.

Hilda pulled her chair closer and peered into Nea's face. 'He? You're sure it's a he?'

'Yes,' Nea shot that off to Hilda before Gregor exploded with wrath.

Gregor's hand gripped the table. 'It got through my wards?' he near bellowed.

Nea nodded, squinting at her grandfather, trying to gauge his level of rage. 'He's not alive so he can slip through our defenses. But he doesn't mean any harm. For some reason, he wants to protect me.' She gave a helpless shrug. 'At least, I think he's not alive. He's not dead. Yet he's not quite a ghost either. He has talent. He can conjure. I was able to talk to him face to face in a setting he devised.'

'What was the nature of the "visitation" you had before you woke drained?' Gregor's expression was stormy, his snowy eyebrows like clouds obscuring his blue eyes.

She swallowed and knew her cheeks flushed. She coughed. Her eyes flicked from Gregor to Hilda and back again. She swallowed. 'Highly sexual,' she said in a strained voice. Then she coughed again and lifted her chin. She'd done nothing to be ashamed of. Even old people had sex, didn't they? 'More adventurous than I could even imagine.'

Hilda nodded, her dark eyes assessing. 'Did he drink from you?'

She coughed into her hand, not able to mistake the other woman's meaning. 'I think so.'

'From where?' Hilda's dark eyes missed nothing.

She couldn't stop her cheeks from burning as her

gaze met the older witch's. She put her cup down, sliding it across the table top. 'I'd rather not say, exactly.' She couldn't look at her grandfather.

After letting out a growl of frustration, Gregor said, 'Don't be shy about it. I've been around the block a few times.'

'I don't care, Grandpa. I can't talk about it with you.'

'Don't call me that. I'm head of the coven; you have to tell me.' When she didn't open her mouth, he sat back, clearly surprised. 'Nea?'

She smacked her hand down on the table. Hilda jumped. 'You're my grandfather. I'm not discussing my sexual encounters with you, not even phantom ones.'

'Right.' Gregor sat back, shrugged, and then targeted the older witch in his sights. 'So, Hilda, what do you make of this?'

The older witch chewed her lip. 'A ghost shouldn't be able to take energy from the living, so we aren't dealing with a real ghost, but I'm thinking that whatever did this isn't quite alive either—not alive as we experience it.'

'A demon then?'

Hilda shook her head. 'I checked for that when I got here. No sign of incubus activity.'

She shivered. She'd not thought of that. 'You can tell?' she asked, quite amazed that Hilda was wise to the cause of her loss of energy, and that she'd surreptitiously checked her out for fraternizing with a demon, and that she was able to look after her without judging her. Her respect for Hilda rose.

'Yes, there are spells that can reveal whether one has been in close consort with a demon. Also—' She tapped her nose. '—I can smell them. Whatever dallied with you it wasn't a demon.'

'He meant me no harm. I read him. I'm sure of it. He said it was accidental.'

'You've met him again?' Gregor bellowed.

'Only for him to apologize, to tell me it was an accident.'

Hilda sniffed. 'Must have been an amazing sexual encounter. He must have sucked from every orifice.' Her eyebrows lifted, and a small smile caused a dimple in her cheek.

Nea's face burned and she covered her face with her hands. Why did Hilda have to say that?

Gregor cleared his throat and his cheeks grew pink. 'Err ... well then.' He rubbed his unshaven chin and cast his gaze around the room. 'I don't like this at all. Although ruling out a demon is a good start.'

Hilda touched her grandfather's arm.

'What?' he responded snappishly.

'I think there is more to it than that ...' She jerked her head in Nea's direction.

Both Hilda and Gregor stared at her, Gregor's fingers strumming the table.

'What?' She asked, shifting in her seat and wishing she was elsewhere.

'How do you feel about this phantom, Nea?' Hilda asked gently.

Nea's eyes widened. Damn that witch for being so perceptive.

Gregor didn't wait for an answer. 'Do you mean she's attached to this creature?'

'He's not a creature, all right? He's a man—a warlock.'

'A warlock? Not a member of my coven, I'll bet!'

She shrugged. 'I never met him before, but he says he's from around here.'

Gregor's eyes widened and his jaw locked.

Hilda nodded. 'Makes sense that he is tied to this place.'

Gregor sent Hilda a warning glance. 'Answer the question, Bethanea.'

'I … I don't know for sure … We have a connection.'

'Do you love this creature?' Gregor didn't do much to hide the derision in his voice.

She wanted to run up the stairs and away from this discussion. How did she feel about Earl? She closed her eyes, remembering her emotions when he'd laid her head on his chest, how at home she'd felt. The love-making was amazing and the things he'd said before that about them being a match? Tears rolled down her cheeks. She shook her head, not sure what she meant to communicate but Gregor could read her heart.

'It's wrong!' Gregor near shouted at her.

'It might not be,' countered Hilda.

Gregor let out a growl, but the other witch didn't flinch.

'She cares for him. Knowing Nea, could she love someone bad, with her reading ability and what you know of her?'

Gregor closed his mouth and shook his head slightly.

'I like him,' she began. 'I don't know if I love him … I mean, there's no hope for a future, is there? He's not really alive.'

The tears fell freely now. She was exhausted and emotionally at sea. Hilda stood up and rubbed her back, making soothing noises.

Gregor picked up his mug and inspected it. He lifted an eyebrow. Hilda sniffed once and took it. She returned with a steaming cup of coffee and plonked it in front of him.

'My granddaughter is in love with a ghost.' He shook his head. 'There's always one in the family. One family member who has to be different, who has to do the unusual.'

'It is not quite right to call him a ghost.' Hilda shared a look with Gregor before meeting her gaze again. 'But there are other states of being—not quite alive, not quite dead.'

Her eyebrows drew together. 'Really? Tell me more.'

Gregor stood up. 'No, she won't.'

Hilda, about to speak, shut her mouth and shot Gregor a nasty look that spoke of hot temper and loud words.

'But ...' she protested.

Hilda patted her hand. 'Later, dear. You know things are never straightforward with the folk. Even animals that live with us take on folk traits. You've heard about Elena's cat, haven't you?'

Nea screwed up her face, trying to recall. 'I don't ...'

'It was undead. It was brought back to life inadvertently by the necromancer, Grace Riordon, when she was just a child. Then, to everyone's surprise, it actually brought itself back to life, flesh-and-blood life. Elena says the cat told her that it found that it could be alive when it had a reason to.'

'Hilda, we need to talk.' Gregor was back to being mean and grumpy.

'We do, hey?' Hilda got up from the table and started rearranging her pots on the bench. 'A while ago you refused to talk to me.'

'That's because I didn't want to talk to you on that topic.'

Hilda started putting her jars away in a big bag,

ignoring Gregor who stood hovering over her. 'And now you expect me to talk to you?'

'Of course! Now I want to talk about what I want to talk about.'

Hilda folded her arms and looked up at Gregor. 'No deal. You answer my questions before we talk about anything else.'

'Or what?'

'I'm going home to my bed. I'm overdue for a nice long sleep in.'

Nea smiled when Gregor growled like a bear. 'Come on then,' he said as he headed for the door. 'In my study.'

Hilda folded her arms and leant her back against the kitchen bench.

Sitting at the table, Nea wanted to demand he share with her too, but had no energy to argue. Hilda glanced at her sideways and hesitated. 'I think we best talk here. Bethanea has a right to know what happened to you, too.'

Pausing, Gregor swung around and he had a no-nonsense expression on his face, all prim mouth and piercing eyes. 'Who are you to tell me what my granddaughter should know?'

Nea nodded approvingly.

Hilda squared her shoulders and lifted her chin, meeting Gregor's glare with one of her own. 'A good friend—to both of you, aye. She told you what had happened to her, although it embarrassed her greatly. You could be just as open as you expect her to be.'

They locked gazes, and then to her surprise, Gregor returned to the table and sat back down. Next he twirled his empty mug. Over his head Hilda winked at her. Nea sat there fascinated. She'd not seen them react this way to each other before. What had happened between them while she'd been bedridden? Was there more meaning to the words going home to my own bed than first appeared? Had Hilda slept with Gregor? At that thought, she sat upright, and paid attention.

'I confronted Penderton.' Gregor spoke in a flat voice. Her skin tingled. 'He overpowered me easily. I'm not sure how. Maybe I was too cocky, too sure of myself. Maybe he had help from her. I only know I just made it out of there in one piece. I had to crawl the last part, being injured as well as partially drained.'

Her mouth hung open. No words came out. What could she say? Gregor had always been the strong one, the leader of the coven, the one people went to, and that upstart, dangerous warlock Drew Penderton, had bested him? She cast her gaze Hilda's way but the older witch said nothing, just nodded sagely as if she'd known all the time.

'So what happens now?' Her brain was having a hard time keeping up with events. She could hardly grapple with the news let alone contemplate any ramifications.

Hilda spoke. 'Gregor has a number of options open to him.'

'Really? What are they?'

'He can resign as leader of the coven—'

'No!' she protested, and then, energy depleted, she sank back into her chair like a rag doll.

Hilda frowned and Nea shut her mouth. 'He can ask for a melding with other members of the coven and go back and confront Penderton again. He can ask for help from the Sydney coven—not too difficult, given Penderton was their problem. Or he can do nothing.'

She glanced from her grandfather to the older woman. Gregor just stared at the mug he was turning around on the spot, not appearing to react at all to the words. 'Grandpa?'

He harrumphed in response and shrugged. 'Don't call me that.'

She shook her head and then shared a pleading look with Hilda.

The older woman leaned over and patted her hand. 'You need to rest a bit more, dear, and your grandpa needs to think.'

'Call me Gregor, why don't you?' He sulked when Hilda just smiled archly at him.

She nodded, glancing uncertainly at her grandfather.

'Up in your room where it's safe, dear,' Hilda said softly.

She eased out of her chair and stumbled to the stairs, feeling like her body was a sack of vegetables that she had to wrestle up the steps. As she put her feet on the risers, low whispers reached her. At least they were talking to each other. Gregor's silences unnerved her. Usually she could go out and get away when he had one of his dark moods. Since her grandmother's death no one had attempted to talk him through them. Hilda was one brave woman.

When she returned to bed, a long-stemmed, pale pink rose appeared, just making itself in front of her eyes. She started and then looked around the room. There was no sign of Earl.

Her gaze went back to the rose he'd conjured on her pillow. A note appeared, a flowery hand wrote: *I'm sorry you are suffering. Forgive me. Earl.*

Her fingertip brushed the tip of a soft velvet petal. It comforted her to know he cared.

Hilda was there the next morning, cooking breakfast when she came downstairs. 'Take a seat, dear. You need to eat before you head out.'

'How did you know I was going out?'

Hilda grinned. 'There's a spring in your step and a glint in your eye. I'd say you'd be wanting to walk around the lake, hey?'

She sat down and poured some coffee. 'Yes, that's exactly what's on my mind.'

She sipped her drink as Hilda turned off the gas and tipped some scrambled eggs onto a plate.

'So how's Gregor this morning?'

'Better,' Gregor said as he lurched into the room. She was confused. He was in better spirits, and he took his plate from Hilda as if it happened every day.

'That's good, then. So what have you decided?'

He glanced up at her and his eyes twinkled. 'Nothing. I'm doing nothing for now.'

'And?' Her gaze flicked between them.

'The council is keeping watch on Penderton and then when we know more, we will act.' This came from Hilda.

'Oh, that sounds good.' She wasn't convinced, but she certainly didn't want her grandfather hurt.

Gregor swallowed another bite of breakfast and then guzzled the remainder of his coffee. 'By the way, I've adjusted the ward. Your phantom lover is locked out.'

'I see.' She understood his caution and wasn't going to argue. There was more going on in the coven than these two were admitting.

Hilda poured more coffee into Gregor's cup and his eyebrows lowered. Something shivered in the air between them. A faint flush crept into his cheeks.

Something more than their romance.

A screech in the ether made her jump up from the table. Hilda dropped the coffee pot and it hit the ground with a bang, splashing dark liquid onto the floor. Gregor lurched out of his seat. It was the house ward. Instead of silently guarding them it was keening.

'What is that?'

'An attack,' Hilda said, heading to the window.

Gregor closed his eyes and then lifted an eyebrow. 'Not your lover boy … it's Penderton.' His eyes widened in surprise and he flinched. 'Ouch! He's made quite a dent in the ward.'

Nea ran to the front door and opened it. A car revved there and when she looked out, an arm reached out of the passenger-side window, flipping the bird at her, and then the car sped off.

Gregor dragged her back and pushed past her into the street. Penderton was gone. Hilda came up beside her and grabbed her hand.

'Don't worry. I've called the other council members. They'll be here soon.'

'It's bad, isn't it?' she asked the older woman.

Hilda nodded. 'Not good. No. Not for Gregor. Not for the coven.'

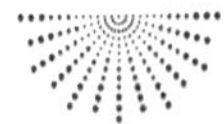

Locked up tight in the house, Nea fretted. She was restless and scared too. It was hard to believe that nasty little creep, Drew, had hurt her grandfather and might possibly attack them further. All day the councillors of the coven had been in the house, talking strategy and allocating watches for Drew. The ward had been reset tighter than before. All because the keening they'd heard earlier in the day had been Drew trying to cut through it. He was playing with them. Gregor had called Rory Penderton, and they had discussed Drew at length. Rory was certain that his son did not have the power to do such a thing when he'd lived in Sydney. After that call, Gregor had announced with certainty that Drew was a dark one and had been trained in the art by Pris Denholm.

The mood was heavy. Nea's heart clenched. Drew's family would be devastated, and she found that she pitied him. She was certain he would never find happiness no matter what he did. Not a happiness that she understood.

Now, looking out over the lake, Nea watched the moonlight on the water, rippling with silver. A man stood on the pier. It was Earl. A sudden surge of need washed over her. She wanted to be with him, wanted to share her concerns. Maybe he would know something or could give her some advice about the young dark warlock.

Turning around, she searched for her robe. Was she seriously thinking of sneaking out to see her phantom boyfriend? Was she that desperate? Bloody oath she was.

Earl was funny, kind, sincere and sensitive—all the qualities she enjoyed in a man. He did things to her that made her body sing. Hopefully this time he wouldn't drain her dry.

As she walked to the pier, her robe flew open, letting the cool night air caress her skin. She was happy for Earl to see her naked. As a witch she had been taught to enjoy life and sex. When they met on the water's edge, her fingers reached for his and he backed away.

'What is it?' she asked.

'I can't be sure I'm not a danger to you.'

'What do you mean? I'm fine. I got better.'

He shook his head and then conjured a scene for them. They were at a table in a restaurant, but they were the only diners. There was no food there, just a single red rose in a slender glass on the snowy table-cloth. The table was too wide to reach across and hold hands. She wanted to get up and go to him, but she couldn't move. She wasn't really there.

'It's too dangerous for you to touch me. There is a threat here, one you can't feel but I can.'

'But that's not coming from you. It's not coming

from making love to me,' she said, and she knew she sounded desperate. 'It's coming from Drew, the new dark warlock.'

'With you weakened, we only invite danger. With you depleted you are vulnerable to the dark one. I have thought about what happened, the risk we took. I could have drained you dry. Unknowingly, you were giving freely to me, and I took. I couldn't help it. I was empty of life. I won't let that happen again—'

'Then we can't make love ever again? Is that what you're saying?' Hot and cold surges rushed through her—anger, fear, love and loss.

He shook his head. 'I don't really know. Maybe when we are over this threat, when the dark one is gone, we can take time to work around it.'

'What do you know about Drew?'

His darkened eyes met hers. 'He's been with Pris. You can't underestimate the danger they represent. Be on your guard. I will do my best to help you.'

'Help me? I don't want your help. I want to make love.'

'I want that too, more than anything, but ...'

She closed her eyes. 'I've never had such an experience. You took me places I've never been. It was glorious, amazing ... Now you say we can't go there again?'

A soft breath caressed her neck and she groaned. A firm presence on her nipples made them contract. 'Just fleeting illusions of touch.'

She was aroused already. Yet looking across the table at Earl she saw all that she wanted but was out of reach. It was back to the self-help manual on sexual fulfillment. 'You can keep your illusions. I want you. I want you now. I don't care about the risk.'

'I care.'

The conjuring faded. She was once again on the shore, her robe open, her skin cool. Earl's presence was fading.

'Please, Earl. Don't leave me.'

'I won't ever leave you …'

The sound of the sliding door opening reached them.

'Nea?' Gregor's voice called out. 'Are you out there?'

Earl's voice lifted on the breeze. 'You'd better go in.'

She bit down on her anger, then nodded and called to the house. 'Yes, Grandpa. Coming in.'

As she gathered her robe around her, she frowned and ground her teeth. Frustration and anger amplified inside her. Denial made the want more. How was she going to cope with reliving their lovemaking knowing it may have been their last encounter?

Her grandfather stood with his arms crossed in the doorway. She grimaced as she walked up the path.

Gregor lectured her. 'What are you doing out there? Why do we have wards? To keep you safe, and you got out there and what?'

'Grandpa, please. I'm okay.'

'You met that phantom lover of yours again. Didn't you?'

'Just briefly.'

'After what he did to you? Are you crazy?'

Her anger built. 'I don't need this right now.' She walked past him and put a foot on the stairs.

'Were you having sex out there, Nea?'

She paused, one hand on the rail, and looked back. Ripe annoyance flooded into her. 'Were you in here?'

'Nea?' Gregor's expression dropped, as if she'd smacked him. 'I don't understand you.'

'Well, what business is it of yours if I slept with Earl on the beach? I'm okay. He didn't mean to hurt me and he didn't this time. I don't ask if you've been having sex with Hilda.'

Gregor swallowed, and his cheeks reddened. 'What has gotten into you? You disrespect me when I'm looking out for you and then hurl accusations.'

She looked down, tears in her eyes. 'I'm sorry. I didn't mean to have a go at you. The pressure is getting to me, Grandpa.' She came back down the stairs and faced him. 'What am I going to do? Earl won't touch me. He doesn't want to hurt me. I feel so bereft. So lost. All I can think about is him touching me, being with me. Of him understanding me and loving me as I love him.'

Gregor grabbed her to him, cradling her head on his shoulder. 'I know it's hard for you. Life is like that sometimes. But in a year's time, things will be different. You'll see, and you'll look back on this and these feelings you have for this phantom lover will have faded.'

She sniffed and pulled back, shaking her head. 'There's a lot of time for anguish between now and then.'

Gregor held her by the shoulders. 'I'm no prude, Nea. Sex is natural and is to be enjoyed. I don't have a problem with you enjoying yourself. But Earl. You said his name was Earl?'

'Yes.'

'I see … well, Earl is not alive and definitely not fit to be your partner in life. We're on alert here. The wards are for your protection. Just be careful. Stay inside them. Okay?'

'Okay. I will. I'm sorry.'

'What else do you know about Earl?'

'He says he grew up around here.'

Gregor nodded, a frown marring his brow. 'Earl,' he repeated, as if savoring a flavor on his tongue.

She lifted her eyebrow in query. "You know of him?"

The old man shook his head. 'It's nothing. Good night.'

She raced up the stairs and took a shower, letting the argument slide away. He only wanted her safe. He wasn't judging her. That had to be Hilda's influence surely. Gregor could be a stickler when he wanted to be.

Earl saw Gregor standing in the garden and knew he was looking for him. There was no point in hiding, so he showed himself to the old warlock. Danger lurked in the shadows, and he had to make the old man understand that he couldn't leave. Couldn't let the dark one take Nea.

'Keep away from her.' Gregor's voice reached him, although he spoke quietly.

'I can't.'

'You must. She belongs with the living.'

'There is danger coming.'

'I will care for her. Leave.'

'No, I won't. She needs me.'

'You will, Earl. You think I don't know you, but I do,' Gregor said, and then followed that up with a thrust of power that threw Earl back. 'Return to whence you came, Earl Pressonville!' Gregor called in that low voice, and he couldn't resist the compulsion. Gregor named him and that gave his thrust sticking power. Before he knew it, he was back in the ground below the ruin.

He had to go back, had to be there. Yet, he could not rise, could not fight the compulsion to stay. He had to wait for the power of Gregor's spell to wane or he'd be drained of power. Tonight he was going to need it.

Too on edge to return to bed, Nea curled up on the sofa with a book. She'd decided it was pointless arguing with Gregor. It had been dangerous to leave the confines of the ward, but she'd been with Earl and there was no harm in that. Definitely no harm, as he wouldn't touch her. There was emptiness inside her where his touch had resided.

Lowering the book, she considered the danger her phantom lover had mentioned and also the hints she'd garnered from what Hilda and Gregor didn't say. Then there was the attack on Gregor, very serious, and now the attack on the ward. What was Drew up to? What did he want? He'd given her the finger and driven off. What was that? A tease? A teenage prank? How big a threat was he?

Even though she tried to dismiss the threat, she couldn't ignore that Gregor had been hiding something before this crisis had emerged. Could it be these dark uprisings that were whispered about here but talked about openly overseas?

With a sigh she put the book aside and went upstairs to go to sleep, then paused. There were alien sounds from her grandfather's room. She stood for a minute and listened, and then understood. He and Hilda were making love and from what she could hear, they were enjoying it. She smiled to herself as she entered her room, lay down and pulled the sheet over her. Go Hilda. Go Grandpa, she thought as she buried her head in her pillow. They should both have smiles on their faces in the morning. She would have to work hard to find hers.

CHAPTER EIGHT

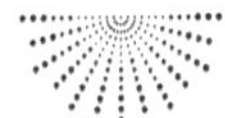

A noise woke Nea. She bolted upright in bed to listen. With a frown, she slid out from under the covers to pull on her robe over her bra and panties. On the landing, she listened hard. Gregor hadn't hailed her and neither had Hilda, so the noise hadn't disturbed them.

That sound again, like a scratching at the window. She slowly descended to the ground floor. It was dark and she groped her way around carefully, not wanting to switch on the light in case she woke the others. Out of the back sliding door she saw that there was no moon, and the lake was liquid night. There was nothing out of the ordinary as far as she could tell.

As she was near the kitchen, she decided to put the kettle on, using the light on the range-hood to find a cup and the tea. The ward was up, she told herself. Nothing to worry about. She was just unsettled. It had to be the wind throwing leaves against a window, that was all.

The disturbance was not repeated. Letting herself grow calm, she poured the water into her mug and added some milk.

With her teacup in hand, she made her way back to the stairs. The scratching sounded again from the front door, louder and sharper than previously. She squinted in the dark. There was a thud. The whole house shook to its foundations. Her tea sloshed onto the carpet as she made to grab the wall to steady herself. Something had hit the house. She reeled. Was that an earthquake?

'Grandpa?'

Still no sound from him. They must have had a good time. Then she detected his awareness and Hilda's, too.

Her mind ran through the possibilities. There were old coal mines in the area and sometimes there had been tremors and even sinkholes appearing—a perfectly rational and non-magical reason for the house to tremble and groan.

Calming down, she tried to soak up the spilt tea with a tissue, and then her feelings of unease grew again. Sending her senses into the land around her, she could detect nothing unusual. It appeared whole. But it had been something. She put her cup and the tea-soaked tissue on the hall table and then went towards the front door.

A door opened behind her.

'Don't!' Gregor called, pulling on a sweater. Hilda had pulled on track pants and an old T-shirt. They started down the hall towards her.

A dull, rhythmic scraping sounded at the front, as if something was trying to dig its way in. She stood and faced the door, a scream begging to climb out of her throat.

The door imploded and she fell back. She heard Gregor's yell and Hilda's scream. Magic crackled around her. Drew was there, looming above her, several men bristling with anger and aggression beside and behind him. In the dazzle, she couldn't tell if they were folk or not. All the power centered on Drew, his sneer ever-present.

'Royston. Feeble old man. Go back to your bed. I've come for Nea, not you.'

Sprawled on the floor in the hall, she asked, 'Me?' She flipped over and scampered back towards her grandfather on her hands and knees.

A rope of power caught her around the feet. 'Stay where you are, whore.'

Gregor thundered out a slap of power. It crackled, and forks of it hit. At first Drew struggled, and then he lifted a hand and flung it back. Repelled, Hilda flew back, hitting her head on the banister before falling unconscious to the floor. Gregor checked her with a quick glance and then stepped forward. 'Keep coming back to me, Nea. I'll not let him take you.'

She tried to move but the dark one's power held her tight. Drew stepped farther down the hall. He'd shredded Gregor's ward. That had to have hurt Gregor, drained his power somewhat.

Drew tilted his head, his dark eyes assessing. 'I see the fabric of you, Royston. Pris was right. You are more bluff than bone.' He made a fist and let go a powerful thrust. She watched her grandfather's body curve as the force hit him and then lifted him to smash against the wall. He sagged, blood trickling down his forehead. She gaped at Drew.

He turned towards her. 'Now you.' His fist of power punched her between the eyes.

A shot of alarm ran through Earl, a zap of electricity making him instantly alert. It took a second for him to register what it was that had stirred him right to the core.

The compulsion spell had evaporated, just like that. Something had happened to the old warlock. He reached out and found the thread of Nea. She was afraid. Her heart raced, and her breathing was ragged. Her mind was filled with shock, with horror, with aversion.

It was but a moment and he was on his way. At the house, Gregor's powerful ward had been cracked open like an oyster shell, a gaping slit through the centre of the house, starting from the front door.

Earl instinctively went to rush forward and then stilled. Voices leaked out the front door, and then he detected movement. The dark warlock came out, with another lesser warlock carrying Nea who was draped unconscious over his shoulders, her arms over her head. A trickle of blood danced on her forehead. The dark one had struck her down.

Rage overcame him, but he banked himself back to nothing but the essence of himself to pass undetected. The dark one looked in his direction, squinting into the night. He stood still, reining in the emotion he'd let surface as he gazed on Nea. He had to work hard to pretend he wasn't there. If the dark one detected and attacked him now, he'd be no use to her.

The dark one looked away and the moment of his demise was postponed. He would survive to help Nea somehow.

He could only watch on in terror as she passed within inches of him and then was bundled into a waiting car. What could he do? He had to get help. That meant making an effort to talk to someone else.

He wanted to follow, but waited. Drew was still there, still scenting the air as if he suspected something. There was nothing he could do on his own. He knew where they were taking her. The dark one was always there, always coming to see Pris, to learn, to steal knowledge, spells, power. He wondered why Pris couldn't see it. Surely after all these years she could see herself in another.

Drew nodded to one of his assistants, the one who had carried Nea's unconscious body. 'Luke, get in the car with her and Jet will drive you to the house.'

With a nod, Luke slid into the back seat of the car, pushing Nea's legs out of his way. A tall, fair-haired man opened the driver-side door and turned the engine over, and the car sped off in a screech of tires. Drew sneered as she was driven away, then he turned back to the house, and a grin quirked the corner of his mouth.

'Now to really fuck with them,' he said to his remaining companion. Earl could see he'd driven a wedge into the ward and levered it apart. It was a strong ward, but the young warlock had found a way around it, bending its power in another direction rather than breaking it down completely. That would have delayed Gregor sensing it but left him with power, unless Drew had other means of draining the old warlock. He'd experienced the old man's power when he'd been banished so it had to be something like that.

He studied the wedge. Theoretically, if it was repaired anyone visiting would be convinced the ward was still doing its job. They wouldn't render aid.

Drew laughed, and the sound chilled him. The

warlock turned to his companion. 'When I've consumed Nea, I'm coming back for the old man. Then I'll be stronger than the old witch. You'll see, Simon.'

'Why not take him now?' Simon urged.

'I'll do him later. I have a night full of plans right now. He isn't going anywhere.'

'You fucked 'em up good.'

Earl was terrified. Drew knew how Pris stayed young and grew her power. He'd been her victim. Drew had followers, those dissatisfied with rules and drawn to someone like him, someone who could provide direction, create havoc, give them satisfaction. This was serious.

Earl picked up Drew's thought: Bethanea Royston so full of life, fit to be drained.

Earl could do nothing by himself, even though every second she spent in Drew's clutches, he ached with worry.

Tension in the air alerted him to the dark warlock sealing up the breach in the ward. He was awed by the skill of it as he hastily placed himself inside its boundaries. From the inside and he guessed outside, too, there was no trace of the breach. That was some feat.

Drew walked off into the night to climb into the car that would take him to Pris's house. Nea was in grave danger. The dark warlock had no love in him. He was an empty space, a void that drew everything inside. He feared that it would extinguish Nea's light and that thought was unbearable. The struggle over what to do was excruciating.

'Come on, Simon. You drive,' Drew said as he opened the passenger door.

The other man nodded, climbed in and revved the engine. He gaped as the car with Drew in it sped off.

A keening sounded erupted from within the

house. It was the older witch. The ward wavered as the power sustaining it faltered.

He sped inside. The older witch was leaning over Gregor, crying and trying to wake him.

Earl conjured an image of himself so she could see him, could talk to him. She tensed, then focused her gaze on him. 'It's you.'

'Yes,' he replied. 'I'm Earl.'

'They've taken her.' She sobbed, clutching at the unconscious warlock. 'Gregor is hurt bad.'

'I know. You must get help. Come now and take her back from him.'

Hilda shook her head, tears dripping from the corners of her eyes. 'There's no time. You must go after them yourself. Save her.'

Panic sped through him, making his conjuring waver. 'How can I?'

Tears sped down Hilda's cheeks, her hands running over the old warlock as she assessed his injuries. 'If you love her, you will find a way. It's been done before. If you're not dead, then you must be alive.'

She can't mean that. I am without substance. Useless!

'Please,' he begged. 'Help Nea. Help me.'

Hilda sobbed openly as she crawled laboriously to the phone. Shaking her head and almost sagging, she lifted the receiver. Puzzled, he listened as she called an ambulance. Why was she so slow? Why wasn't she helping him? Then when that call was done, she called one of the other councillors, her voice low and feathery. She was using all of her will to keep talking, to make her instructions clear. It was taking too long.

Hilda lay down on the floor and looked up at him, her cheeks sagging and her eyes closing with fatigue. 'Why are you still here?' she said, her voice barely above a whisper.

'I can't save her on my own. You must come to Pris's house.'

'I can't. He drained me.' Her fingers walked to Gregor's hand and held it. 'Go, please. Go now. Help Nea.' Then her eyes closed. 'I'll send the others when they come.'

He had no choice. He had to try. Inside, his anger and frustration warred together. This shouldn't be happening. There should be others more able than him to rescue her. He would not wish his fate on anyone, least of all his beautiful Nea.

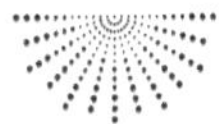

CHAPTER NINE

Earl was at Pris's house, out on the street. The usual defensive wards were down. This gave him pause. Were they down because Drew had torn them down or because those inside wanted to pretend that no one was there? No cars were out front. Maybe his followers had dropped them, rather than joining in with the ritual. There was no time for hesitation. A delay could be the difference between life or death.

On the porch, he looked for a way in. There was a gap in the seal in the window; the whole house was rundown. Surely Pris lived somewhere else and used this place for rituals these days.

As he slid through the cladding and the window frame, he entered the dank front room. Water damage patched the ceiling with brown stains and spots of rotting carpet revealed bare floorboards beneath. It had been cosy and whole in his time. His gaze passed over the tapestry-covered armchair and matching chaise, the upholstery had holes and was smattered with black mould stains.

Moving to the hallway, he made his way to the back of the house, ignoring the crumpled newspapers and the skittering feet of mice as they scrambled out of his way, reacting to his presence even though he wasn't there, not really there. He knew where to go. He knew the door that the stairs hid behind. It was the last place he wanted to be.

He dared not reach out with his talent in case the dark folk detected it. He thought perhaps Drew had done so near Gregor's house but couldn't be sure. Thank the Goddess that Hilda had been able to speak with him within his conjured image, because he was invisible otherwise. He was so insubstantial he should be able to pass unseen by those with the talent provided he kept himself controlled. Drew had talent. Too much of it, but he had to risk it.

He slid down the stairs, his presence not making the decaying wood creak. Light leaked from under the door. It was the door to the place where his life had ended. He couldn't stop, even though it held a confronting memory—the moment of his greatest mistake, the moment his life had ended. Having to face it, he passed through.

In the basement room, with walls draped in faded red fabric, sat the back of the old-fashioned dentist chair. A shudder ran through him at the sight of it. As he moved around the room, he saw that an unconscious Nea lay there, her shoulders, hands, waist and ankles strapped down.

There was movement and he turned, catching sight of the men coupling. Drew's chest was bare and he did up his fly as he pulled out of the other man. Luke, who had accompanied the young warlock earlier, fell forward to lay across the floor, naked and with blood welling from a small cut to his throat. Totally absorbed in his ritual, the warlock didn't even look in Earl's direction. Drew's chant hung in the air as he knelt and sucked at the man's blood, draining the life force from the younger, weaker warlock. The victim moaned, struggled feebly, trying to push his attacker away. The dark warlock grabbed him by the hair and wrenched his head back, causing the wound to gape open. Rich blood pumped out and Drew slurped at it loudly, hungrily.

Earl could taste the power of the blood, and the words of the ritual that hovered in the air that bound together to feed the dark one. Life drained from the young warlock. Death lurked in his grey eyes and pale cheeks and in his stilled expression—half agony, half fear.

Drew had stolen Pris's ritual. He'd lured this warlock by some means, seduced him, and then stolen his life. Nea was trussed and ready to be his next victim.

Drew was already powerful. Sucking Nea's life force would make him unstoppable. Unlike Pris, who used it to stay young, Drew had other plans. He was darker even than the old witch. He had a purpose—a deadly purpose.

Overcome with horror, Earl backed away, the scene before him sparking flashbacks to his own demise. He couldn't fight this. He just couldn't. Drew was already too powerful. Hilda had to be crazy to think he could. His gaze rested on Nea, on her still face, her freckled button nose and pale pink lips. Lips he longed to kiss. The blonde of her hair draped over the side of the chair, a finger of blood staining one side. He couldn't fight this.

Drew lifted away from his victim, wiping his mouth with the back of his hand. He was even stronger now. His flesh glowed with power. Earl was sick to his heart to see it.

Unable to stop himself, he peered into the dead warlock's flesh. He was definitely fully drained.

There was nothing left as there had been with himself. For a moment, he thought that maybe Nea would live like him after the dark one drained her and could join him in his half-life. They'd be together forever. He'd no longer be lonely. The idea was tantalizing and seductive, but there was no guarantee she'd be like him, alive but not alive. His own survival had been a fluke. Pris hadn't noticed that part of him lived before she threw his corpse away. There had been no others like him in the intervening years.

Drew was more likely to end her completely. There was a thoroughness to the warlock that left him in little doubt. She wasn't even conscious. How could she fight him like that?

He remembered that night, when the dark witch had drained him of life. Pris had used him, taking him to the edge of ecstasy—kisses soaked in power, washing over him like a drug. He was too young and too blind to see what she was doing. It was all about his cock, the intense knot of pleasure she unlocked, piece by piece, but taking his will with each burst of passion, with each degree of increase in pleasure. He had been obsessed with her—the power, the beauty, the sex. She'd lifted a finger and he'd come crawling. She'd tied him up and whipped him until he'd begged for more. The images and memories flooded into him.

Earl retreated slowly to a dark corner of the room, drawing his essence in and quieting himself, wary that any swift movement would attract attention. Drew would be distracted while absorbing the other warlock's power, but also the ritual would have honed every sense, every nerve, every tendril of his talent.

Hunched over, the dark warlock wept as he absorbed the power from his victim, incorporating it into his flesh. His naked upper body shuddered and writhed. Then he cried out as he tugged the very last bit of essence into himself, culminating in a climax that left him sweating and gasping and his eyes rolling up in his head.

While Drew was still exhilarating in his new power, Nea came to. Her hands jerked, then her foot twitched. Her head rolled from side to side. Earl had prayed she would stay unconscious. He would not like to feel her terror or have her experience what he had gone through.

If he had tears they'd be flowing right now. *Oh Nea. I'm so sorry I can't protect you.* He reached outside, trying to see if any members of the coven were close, whether help was on its way. But there was nothing. Nea was alone except for him.

The thought of her bright light absorbed by such a dark one made him tremble down in his soul. He was surprised he could still say he had one but he did. He feared for her.

Earl's anger speared into him. *Oh, that I wasn't a useless remnant of my former self. I'd crush this boy, this upstart drowning in his own darkness.*

Suddenly, she screamed. The young warlock had not bothered to gag her. Her head jerked around as she struggled, trying to kick her legs and twist her arms free. Being strapped to that dentist chair restricted her movements. Energy crackled around her.

'Awake just in time, sweeting.' Drew brandished a knife, the ceremonial blade. Blood caked the edge. It was the one he'd used to slay the other warlock. Earl was in despair.

Drew parted Nea's robe, and cut the bra she was wearing so that her pale breasts were exposed. 'All the better to see you with,' he said as he licked along her sternum. 'All the better to drain your power.'

She struggled, thumping her legs, trying to push off the straps that tied her. 'Let me go, you freak.'

'Shut up or I'll cut your tongue out. Maybe I'll take what you didn't give me before.' He tugged the robe farther apart. She had underpants on. He lifted the elastic and stabbed his fingers between her legs.

'No,' she cried. 'You'll not touch me, you creep.'

She let loose her power. Drew was shoved back, his head jerking sideways from the virtual slap. But his eyes flashed. 'Luke liked to fuck. He begged me for a fuck while you lay there, unconscious. I thought maybe I'd try the ritual out on him first. It worked. You like to fuck. Don't you?' he said knowingly.

'Fuck off, you creep,' she hissed at him, arching her body as she fought against the restraints.

'That's not nice. I'm offering you a bit of satisfaction before you die.' He shrugged. 'I'm thinking the ritual will work whether I'm fucking you or not. I can always fuck you while I'm draining you. Sex brings your power to the surface—did you know that? The greater the desire, the more heated your talent becomes.'

He lashed out with his magic, holding her immobile while his hand went to her throat. 'I can strangle you right here and now.' He squeezed tighter. 'I can fuck you while you look on and can do nothing. Let your family try to save you. Let them watch while I savor their despair as the one they came to save dies.'

She threw her head from side to side. 'Gregor!'

'You think granddaddy is going to come for you?' he whispered harshly into her face. 'The old man was like a piece of soft cheese. Pris told me what his weakness was, where the kink in his defenses were. He's down and out, little one. He's not coming. He's probably dead. No one is going to save you.'

'They will. They will find me and kill you.' She spat at him.

'Pris didn't think I'd use that information. It was a silly boast, done to impress me. I told her that Gregor was trying to be "nice" to me. She doesn't really know that you exist really.'

'No ...' She tugged harder against the restraints. The straps cut into her skin. Drew licked the blood there.

'Keep it up and I won't have to use the knife. I'll just chant the words and suck the life ever so slowly out of you.'

'No ...' This time, she cried in despair. She was giving up. Earl wanted to let her know he was there. Not that he was any use. Not that he could help, but she would know she wasn't alone. Yet, if Drew detected him, the dark warlock would extinguish him for sure.

'I fuck Pris, and I flatter her, and she's grateful for my cock, and she tells me things and I pretend to be ignorant. That witch has no imagination. Even less than you have, I think.'

There was a shift in power, a dark ripple that left a familiar taste in his mouth.

He turned and fell back in surprise. It was Pris on the stairs. A dark lace robe barely covered her nakedness. She was still as beautiful and young as she'd been when she'd drained him. Fear and rage near overwhelmed him. His gaze shifted, and Drew stiffened.

'What the fuck do you think you're doing, Drew Penderton?'

Drew whirled, his hand withdrawing from Nea. 'My dark lady.' He bowed his head, his hand still holding the knife hidden behind his back.

Pris's eyes blazed as she took in the dead body

with the cut throat in the corner. Her robe swirled as she swung towards him. 'You killed in my house? How dare you! That is my privilege.' She kicked the dead body out of her way. Sniffed around it. Took in the naked form, the dried blood. Her shoulders straightened as she tasted the remnants of the spent energy around the body. Then she turned to Drew, mouth agape. Then, pursing her lips, she said, 'You could not have done this.'

Drew kept his head bowed, pretending meekness. Earl banked himself back so he was barely there.

Pris's gaze then settled on the occupant of the chair. 'The Royston girl. What is the meaning of this? You have broken the agreement I have with Royston. She is his.' She walked forward and Drew stepped away, leaving Nea for the dark witch to inspect. Her gaze was searching, her nostrils flaring. She ran a hand along Nea's mid line, her gaze assessing the girl's nakedness. She licked her lips. Earl suspected she was calculating how she could turn this situation to her advantage.

A hopeful look sprung into Nea's eyes. It broke his heart to see it. 'Please,' Nea begged. 'Let me go.'

Pris's pale hand lifted to Nea's chin, and she inspected her face. 'Not beautiful.' She drew her hand down to Nea's vulva, cupping her. 'But young. Full of life.'

The dark witch turned to face the young warlock. Pris would take her life just as Drew would. If anything, Pris was calculating how she could drain Nea and blame it on Drew. 'How did you steal it?'

'What?' Drew said, shrugging, his face expressionless.

'Don't,' she hissed, seeming to grow taller and more menacing. Drew cowered before her but Earl sensed there was something not right about it. He tried to get a measure of their power. Drew's throbbed. Pris's was hidden. He didn't like it. 'Lie. To. Me. You stole it.'

'What?' Drew said again, this time not quite able to hide his amusement. There was a dangerous twinkle in his eye.

Pris strode forward but Drew stepped sideways, keeping the distance between them as they circled one another. She pointed to Nea, who still desperately struggled against her bindings. 'Do you think I'm stupid? I can taste it in the air. You have her ready for sacrifice. You have stolen the spell. Give it back.'

'I can't.'

It was then the old witch made a decision. He saw it in how her expression closed down, her eyes hooded, her mouth drawn in tight. Her power was hidden but she couldn't hide her intention. She was readying to strike, and Drew let her. Drew fell and sprawled on the ground, the knife falling a bare inch or two from his hand. He was stunned and unmoving. Earl could hardly think. What would Pris do? Would she let Nea go? He thought not. Not when the prey was set before her like that, no matter what agreement she had with the old warlock, Gregor. She could blame it all on the dark warlock, who was out of control.

She stepped up to the chair and smiled down. 'There, there. Did that nasty warlock scare you?' She smoothed Nea's hair and she grew still. 'Silly boy. He doesn't realize that the ritual works better when the victim is at peace, sated, surrendering.'

He knew there was a problem now. Pris was singing, casting a net of calmness over her captive, fudging Nea's brain so that she didn't know her danger and thought Pris was rescuing her, but Pris was getting ready to take her life. One dark one had been replaced by another.

Pris sucked on one of Nea's breasts. 'Do you like that?' she crooned, as if to a child. 'I can promise you ecstasy. Fulfillment. You want me to fuck you, don't you?'

Nea whimpered. Earl sensed she was fighting the dark witch's spell. Pris's voice rose in pitch, the words swimming through the air. Nea sighed.

'There, there, rest now, my sweet,' Pris said and kissed Nea, first a peck on the forehead and then her tongue speared into Nea's mouth. Nea's body arched, but Pris held her chin so she couldn't fight. Stupor relaxed Nea's muscles. 'That's right, relax. Give yourself to me, Gregor's little grandchild. How tasty you will be. Although you're tainted by human blood your energy will taste nice. Strong warlock, with strong magic. His power runs through your veins.' She twisted Nea's nipple, drawing it to a bud. 'Yes. So full of desire.' Her fingers dove into Nea's cleft and began stroking. 'Come for me, sweet thing. It's been so long since I've had a woman.'

Pris lathed Nea's breasts with her tongue, then lifted her head to fill the air with her chanting. This went on for a minute, maybe two, until as if just remembering something, Pris stilled. Lifting her head, she noticed something was different in the room and turned suddenly, her gaze sweeping the floor. Drew wasn't there; neither was the knife.

Earl had been so caught up with what Pris was doing to Nea that he had missed the fact that Drew had moved.

There was a change in the shadows and Pris tensed. 'What?' Pris's head jerked up and she scanned the ground where Drew had lain. 'Where are you,

you little snake? Don't think you can escape from me.'

She clawed the air, commanding Drew forward. Earl was nearly caught in the summoning.

From the shadows Drew surged forward and drove the knife in her chest. Taken by surprise, the dark witch didn't even try to ward him off. The old witch was flung back, her arms splayed as she lay over Nea, her naked breasts pointing to the ceiling. Pris's hands reached up and pulled the knife out. Blood spurted from the wound as she stared at the blade and patted at the wound with her other hand as if to stop the blood leaking out of her. Her hand came away with more gore on it. Gaping, she stood up and shrieked. The blade fell from her fingers as she took a faltering step, another and then fell.

The blood pouring from the wound had a life of its own. Energy wafted off it. Earl could taste it, was drawn to it. That was his life in that blood. It was what she had taken from him all those years ago, except then she had fucked him, confused his mind with sex so that he hadn't seen it coming. That was why it was his own fault. This moment was happening because of a mistake he made so many years ago. He should have died, but he didn't.

He wasn't sure why, but he was drawn to the blood, to the life force leaking out of Pris. It called to him, beckoned his essence. It was his life, his energy. He should take it back. The pulse of it throbbed, calling to him, reaching out.

The dark warlock didn't take any notice of the power leaking out of the dying witch. Stepping over Pris, Drew chanted now as he hovered over Nea. He was going to do the same to Nea, take her life force, take it into himself, building his own power at her expense. She'd most likely die, or end up like him, neither dead nor alive.

Earl gazed upon her, then at Drew's rapturous expression. He was slavering over her, waiting impatiently to sup of her energy. He undid his fly.

'I'll do it her way then. I can see she has lowered your barriers.' He rubbed at Nea's cleft and she moaned.

Earl shuddered with rage. It could not be. It should not be. Yet, he could not do anything. Not like this, not a specter.

He had to save her.

Blood still pumped out of the dying witch. It was as if he could taste the salty tang of it. It curled into tendrils wending their way out into the air before her. He could feel them, reaching out. Drew was too intent on molesting Nea to notice the dark witch. He was letting all that dark magic go to waste, all of Pris's life force trickle away.

Drew's chanting reached a peak. He lowered the chair and climbed on. He had one hand on the knife, the other on his cock, rubbing it to hardness. The blood-stained knife glistened in his hand.

He had to act now. Instinctively, he plunged himself into the rich blood leaking from the downed dark witch, letting the tendrils of power connect with his essence.

At contact, there was an immediate reaction. Her power surrounded him and then welcomed him. Without even thinking about it, he drew the power into himself. He remembered who he was and what he was made of and the powers wove together, taking the blood to remake the flesh.

The verses of the ritual fell around his head, each word striking like a knife. He needed to use this power to drive off Drew, but it wouldn't go where he wanted it. Some spell was at work, weaving the dark witch's power around his essence, his body.

Drew paused in his chanting, a natural break between stanzas as he parted Nea's legs, his gaze totally intent on his victim. Then his voice rose as he began the last chorus to bring the ritual to the end.

Earl's heart beat frantically. His breaths came in loud huffs. He was breathing. He thought he was breathing. He shook his head to clear it. Nea didn't put up a fight. Pris had calmed her, and now only whimpers leaked from her lips. Her eyelids were lowered over her lust-filled eyes.

Power washed over him, making his knees buckle. The words falling from Drew's mouth were winding themselves around Earl, around Pris's blood. Earl's memory engaged and he pictured himself how he was. His life ran into him as the old witch's essence released its power. He was being remade as he watched the blade hover above Nea's chest. He had to stop it. Had to.

At last, a scream erupted from her lips. It cut into his soul. The warlock was positioned, his stiff cock in his hand. Her eyes were wide as she gaped at the blade held aloft, anticipating the killing blow.

He would give his life for her. Intent on shielding her, he surged forward. He thrust his shoulder into Drew's chest, knocking him to the floor. The blade glanced her upper arm, a shallow cut, no more.

Drew yelled, rage dripping from his features as he hunched over, pulling his trousers up. 'Who the fuck are you?' He balled his fists now that he was re-housed. 'And where the fuck did you come from?'

Standing still, he blinked. 'You can see me?' Being alive was still a new sensation.

Drew looked around him as if he needed confirmation that he was talking to an idiot. 'Of course I bloody see you. Now get out of the way.'

He stood firm, his shoulders back. 'No, I won't let you hurt her.'

'You'll regret his.' Drew pushed him with his power.

He rocked back but kept his feet. He looked down. He had substance. He had form. He breathed—his chest rose and fell. He was alive. The wonder of it distracted him. He had to focus. This was for Nea. He was alive for her. To save her.

'I don't care who you are. Just get out now and I'll let you live.' Drew gestured, but he anticipated him. He'd been a fair warlock in his youth; now, after years of contemplation and a new body, he was an easy match for this young warlock and all his posturing. He deflected the powerful blow, and with a quick flick of his hand sent it back.

Drew's dark eyes were wide with surprise and he failed to defend himself. The blow hit, sending a rebounding shockwave over Earl. It rippled his hair. Earl touched his head, felt the strands. He had hair again. The wonder of his re-embodiment had him reeling.

Drew lifted up and flew backwards. He landed on the warlock he had killed. Groaning, he tried to roll to his feet, shaking off the blow.

Wasting no time, Earl tugged at the straps, trying to free Nea. He slapped her gently on the cheeks. 'Nea? Get a grip. We have to get you out of here. Nea?'

He used a spell, sending a spike into her brain. Her eyes snapped open and she gasped.

'What? Who?' She blinked a few times. 'Earl?' Her eyes were bright with tears. She reached out and touched his cheek. 'You're real?'

'Yes. No time to explain.' He continued undoing the straps. She started helping. A movement behind him—a ripple of power alerted him to Drew readying to attack. 'I'll free you in a minute,' he said as he turned to confront the attacking warlock.

The dark warlock sprang at him. Earl caught a fist to the chin and went down, bringing the warlock with him. Hooking his hands so that he dragged Drew along. Tangled together, they rolled on the floor. Drew gouged at his eyes, kneed him and tried to bite. Earl was hard pressed to separate from his enemy so that he could grab hold of his talent and shove him away. He was unused to his own physical being. It had been so long since he'd had arms and legs and strength.

Drew's fingernail scraped down Earl's face. It hurt. Instinctively, he lashed out with his power. Drew was thrust up into the air, straight through the ceiling to the floor above. Timber floorboards came crashing down. Earl covered his head, but a falling piece of timber dazed him.

Vulnerable, he expected Drew to come at him again. Those were anxious moments while he waited, but there was nothing.

Pushing the fallen floorboards off, the sound of weeping reached him. His pale skin was bloody and raw in places. He had cuts, and a sizable wood splinter sticking out of his thigh. He lay there, gaping. It hurt. The full realization hit him. He had a body. He was alive.

Nea tugged at the remaining straps. Now she was more alert, she used her talent to help her loosen them. Gingerly, Earl climbed to his feet, careful of the wound he'd garnered when the ceiling had exploded.

Above, the sound of footsteps came rushing towards the gaping hole. Earl froze. Was that Drew coming back? His heart leapt. He positioned himself to protect Nea. Even with an injury he still had plenty of talent left. It rippled under his skin, a hot, cleansing sensation.

Readying himself, he let out a breath when a head peeped down from the hole in the floor. It wasn't Drew but a stranger. Still wary, he reached out with his talent. From the feel of the newcomer, he was a warlock and friendly. One of Gregor's coven, he guessed.

'Goddess! What the hell happened here? Looks like we missed the party.' The head pulled up and the councillor called out to someone else. 'Call the rest of the council. We're going to need help to get them out.'

Relief leaked out of Earl. It was going to be okay. Nea was safe. Pris was dead and Drew ... he frowned. Where was Drew?

Nea climbed out of the chair, holding her robe together over her breasts. After sending her gaze around the room, her eyes settled on Earl and widened. Her pink tongue moistened her parted lips, and there was wonder and questioning in her expression.

The head came back. 'Hello, Nea. What are you doing down there?'

Nea broke eye contact and tilted her head up. 'Hi, Humphrey,' she said in a low voice. 'It's good to see you.'

'Don't worry, dear. Hilda sent us word that you were in trouble. Gregor is still out of it, but doing okay. With all the talent being expended around here, it didn't take us too long to find you.' He looked from one end of the basement to the other. 'I make two dead. That sound about right?'

'Yes,' Nea said as she took in the two dead bodies: Pris and the warlock who'd helped abduct her.

'And what about you, Bethanea? You look well, but are you all right?'

Her hand drew back the hair out of her eyes and she studied the room absently. 'Yes, I think so … a bit lightheaded … a bit … bruised.' She touched her arm where she'd been sliced by the dagger. 'A small cut. Not too bad.'

'Very well. We will check you over soon. Help will be here momentarily.'

Earl hobbled a little closer.

'Is … is Drew Penderton's body up there?' Earl asked, the sound of his voice surprising him.

Humphrey's eyes widened. 'Who are you, mate? And why are you naked?'

Earl glanced up and then down. He tilted his head to the side. He was rather impressively naked. 'My name is Earl.'

Humphrey bristled, his eyes narrowing. 'Can't say that I've heard of you.'

Earl detected the build-up of talent. Humphrey was a medium-level enforcer from what he could detect.

'It's okay,' Nea said in a weak voice. 'He saved me. I can vouch for him. Can you look for a body up there?'

The momentary hostility in Humphrey's eyes lessened and with a nod he went away. The sound of movement echoed within the basement and after a few minutes he returned. 'No bodies up here,' he replied. 'Are you missing someone?'

Earl furrowed his eyebrows together. 'Yes, Drew, the dark warlock. He took a blow …' Earl gestured the ceiling. 'And ended up there.'

'A mighty blow that must have been. A kill strike?'

He nodded. 'It was strong enough to kill. Necessary to save Nea.'

Again Humphrey's eyes assessed him and Earl detected the calculation behind them. A faint prickle on his skin let him know that the councillor was trying to assess his talent and the danger he represented.

Nea's mouth dropped open and she let out a small sound of surprise. Earl drew in closer to her, ready to catch her if she was faint or support her if needed.

'It is really you,' Nea said, her eyes traveling all over him. There was an eagerness and a hunger in her eyes, yet her expression held wariness as if she were dreaming. With a glance at Humphrey, she started searching on the floor for something. Then she walked to the wall and tugged down some fabric that hung there and passed it over. Mesmerized, he took it from her and wrapped it around his hips, avoiding the protruding piece of wood that jutted from his thigh.

'Thank you,' he whispered.

'Goddess, you're hurt.' She leaned down to inspect the splinter. 'I didn't notice before with ... um ...you being naked.'

'It's nothing.' His cheeks were burning. What a feeling it was to blush. Really blush?

Their gazes met and she bit her bottom lip, ready to speak. 'But there's blood and ...'

'Truly. It's a minor injury. You, though, took a blow. You should be seen to first.'

Nea didn't smile and the way she tensed her jaw indicated to him that she was in pain. He glanced at her eyes and saw the headache there. He wanted to reach out and soothe her, tell her it was going to be all right.

More footsteps echoed above their heads. Humphrey called out to his companions, 'Be careful, the supports are compromised. I'll hold them up while you climb down with the stretcher.' He lowered his head to speak to them. 'A healer is on the way.' He looked at Earl. 'And maybe we can find some clothes for you too, sir. It won't be long.'

Nea looked at him, lifting a hand to touch his face but hesitating. 'It is you.' A wondrous smile broke out on her face, sweeping away the signs of pain. He'd never seen a better sight in all his life. 'You saved me,' she whispered. 'I don't know how—'

Her tentative hand touched his chin, then she lifted her fingers and swept the curls off his forehead. 'Goddess!' Her voice was tinged with wonder. 'I feel your warmth, your sweat ...'

His skin tensed and his heart throbbed painfully. Closing his eyes, he sighed. Nea was touching him for real. The friction of her fingertips sent spikes of electricity into his mind, the sensation potent and liquid. His knees were ready to crumble, a sob threatened to escape his tight throat, and the tears that brimmed in his eyes tracked down his cheeks.

'You are flesh and blood. So warm and alive and powerful. May I?' she asked, the blue of her eyes dark pools in the dimly lit room.

Her hands trailed across his shoulders and down his arm. His arousal was instant. Drawing her hand to his center line, she traced the shape of his nipples then down his pecs to where the material covered him like a kilt. Trembling followed in the wake of her touch. Her gaze shifted to his face and then she traced her forefinger across his bottom lip. Her exhale was drawn out and full of damp promise. Stepping closer, light suddenly glistened in her blue eyes and her smile was radiant. She liked what she saw.

Hope and love flickered inside his chest. His heartbeat sped up. He gloried in life and in touch. Because of her he had life. One touch from her and his body had responded, his love ripened to a life bond so strong he didn't think it could wane in a million years.

Then she stepped closer to enter the circle of his arms, making sure she did not brush against his injury, and lay her head on his right breast. Her face was cool against his warm skin and yet his breath hitched at the contact. Her hair fanned out along his skin, tickling and teasing in a way that was tantalizing and familiar. Trembling, he leaned down and kissed the top of her head. Having her there felt so right.

'Earl?' She gazed up at him. 'This is where I belong. Just here. Just this spot.' She then rubbed her face against his bare skin and emotion and arousal came together in a rush. She must have noticed because she pressed against his side and groaned softly. He was too surprised and mortified to comment on his body's reaction. Time enough for that when they got out of there.

Her read of him was natural and instinctive and he made no move to block her. He wanted no secrets between them. Opening himself up, he detected when she sampled the lonely years when he'd dwelled beneath the ground and the bitter regret that had imbued him and then reshaped his soul. He travelled with her through his memories. Like sunlight on a deep, dark pond, the experience of her reaching out and touching him was relived together. Her mind widened at the wonder of it, of what it meant to him and how it had changed him. That night her touch had been as light as a butterfly, eliciting a flicker of hope that had grown inside him, essentially shaping his essence into something new, something good, something that wanted to live. He was there because of her. He owed his life to her.

With a gasp, she withdrew from him and staggered, her hand clutching her head. He steadied her with his hand, and their eyes met. 'I don't know how you bore it. I will never understand it, or this.' She patted his skin.

In the next breath, her face drained of color suddenly.

'Nea?' he said as his arm circled her waist to support her.

Her hands started to shake and she gaped as she held them in front her. 'I feel strange—'

He caught her as she fainted. He swept the hair from her forehead as he looked down at her. There was bruising on her face from where she'd been struck. He hoped it was that and not something she'd read in him that had caused her to pass out. Then he cursed himself for a fool for being so selfish. Carefully, he inspected her for any hidden injury. Coming to, she mumbled and could say her name but was still disoriented and woozy.

'Hey, Humphrey. You better hurry. Nea has passed out.'

Humphrey came back. 'They are coming now. Won't be long.'

CHAPTER TEN

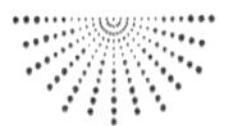

Nea threw herself into Earl's arms and rested her head on his chest. Heartbeats thrummed below her ear, and the warmth radiating from him bathed her with comfort. He was alive—living, breathing alive. *Goddess! How could he be?* Yet, the tangible evidence proved that he was indeed alive and she was in his arms.

Earl being alive was beyond any expectation that she'd had. It took some readjusting. Not in an unpleasant way, but more that she had to now open herself up to possibilities of a future, of what might be, of what could be. As she nestled there, it was as if she was home. This was where she was staking her claim. He was a living, breathing warlock. His touch would no longer drain her of energy. Her mind sang at the thought.

The read of him revealed long years of remorse and she understood how that had shaped who he was now. She honored him for his thinking—although he had dwelt in darkness, it did not inhabit him. He longed for light, for life, and he had allowed the touch of her mind to draw him out. In the days she had known him, he'd been trying to protect her.

Now, he had done the unimaginable. He'd used the blood magic to win himself back to life and he'd done it to save her life, to prevent her from suffering his fate. Surely that had to count for something, even though it was still blood magic.

She trembled as she contemplated what came next. She had figured out that the future was not going to be easy. The coven would judge him and her too. They had to be free of the dark witch's taint, and how could they prove that they were? Then there was the fact that Drew was still out there. Closing her eyes, she pushed those thoughts away and focused back on the moment.

As her gaze ate up the sight of Earl, of him in the flesh, she knew she didn't want to lose him. Yet, there was a possibility that everything would unravel. What if tomorrow he was gone? What if this body was only temporary? She ran her hands over him, comforting herself that he really was real. That his body was warm and solid and alive. She had to believe that he was here to stay.

She pulled away gently so that she could look at his face. He didn't stop her. She had a lump on her head, and the aftertaste of a hex on her tongue. It was hard to concentrate with him so close, with him in the flesh. Breaking eye contact, she cast her gaze around the room.

A light blazed overhead, lowered by Humphrey, and the state of the room was revealed. Torn draperies, Pris's body stiff now, her face drawn with aged wrinkles, the semblance of youth erased. The younger warlock lay with his head to the side, his cut throat gaping like an extra mouth.

She rubbed her upper arms, suddenly chilled. She knew it could have been her lying dead. If not for Earl.

'You risked a lot to save me. I see that. Your essence was fragile, easily extinguished,' she told him.

'I would have given myself freely to prevent you ending up dead or like me. Yet, with no body, I had no chance of being any real help. Beautiful Bethanea, because of you I was awakened and because of you I live.'

The words warmed her and she found it hard to look away from his captivating eyes. 'What was he going to do to me? I don't understand how killing me was helping him. He was already young, so he didn't need me for that. Not like Pris.'

'Blood magic. Dark magic. It's dangerous and seductive. He was going to take your life, use your blood to grow his power.' His voice sounded so rich in her ears. It was similar to his conjured voice, but had more depth.

Her heart quaked. She noticed his eyes then, a hazel brown with green and yellow lights, just like he looked in his conjuring. 'How do you know that? Are you a dark one?'

'No, not a dark one, but one who has been touched by the dark. It was Pris who attracted me. I knew I was doing wrong in coming to see her, for wanting her, but I was too blind to see. With your energy in me, I found that I could hear Drew's thoughts at times. That is why I knew the danger.'

She gaped at him. 'You knew Pris? It was she who I saw in your past? The one you loved, the one who betrayed you?'

He sighed. 'I was infatuated with her, Nea. Obsessed. Not love. I didn't know any better. I wasn't truly dark, just randy as all hell.' He closed his eyes and then opened them again, tears welling at the edges. 'I flirted with the dark without even thinking about it. I'm sorry. I am so unworthy.'

She glanced at the old witch and nodded. 'You fucked that old hag?' The revulsion surged inside her.

He nodded. 'Except she wasn't an old hag then, she was young and beautiful, and I fell for her trap. It was only the once you know. She killed me, took my life force …'

She was overwhelmed. 'I can't take this in.' She shook her head.

The healer, Siv, dropped to the floor. 'Who shall I look at first?'

She suggested Earl and Earl said for her to be seen to first.

'That's not very helpful.' Siv glanced at Earl and then at her. 'You first. Head injury and possibly shock.'

She'd never been treated by Siv before, him being relatively new to the coven after moving to the area from India with his wife and three children.

Siv urged her to sit on the floor and squatted down next to her, then he grew still as he used his talent to assess her injuries. 'Some bruising. The brain appears whole.' His hand gently touched her forehead. 'A slight concussion, nothing too serious. We can probably take you home.'

'How is Gregor? Is he at home yet?'

Siv's lips drew into a line and his gaze flicked to Earl. She didn't have to read him to know that it wasn't good news. 'He's in the hospital at the moment. But I believe he'll be okay. Right now, I think we'll get you home and then you can take it from there, okay?'

'What about Earl?' she said. Her hand itched to reach out to him just to confirm that his flesh was real. 'I don't want to leave without him.'

Siv moved his head from side to side, a uniquely Indian gesture. 'Very well then. I suppose you'll do.'

He stood up and cast his gaze over Earl. 'Now let's look at you.'

Siv used his talent, nodding as he examined him. 'Interesting. I've never seen someone so healthy. There are no flaws in you at all, no wear and tear, no aging.' Siv's gaze centered on the wood sticking out of Earl's leg. 'Mmm,' he said as he sealed up the scratch on Earl's face and his other minor grazes. 'That's about it for your injuries. Now if you will lean against this chair, I can probably extract that bit of wood.'

Earl did as he was instructed.

Siv sent a wave of talent into Earl's leg, then he assessed the injury more closely. She could see that he was separating the flesh from the splinter. Then before she could blink, he had the splinter out and the wound sealed up. 'You should be fine now. A bit tender for a day or so.' Siv glanced up at her. 'Are you okay? Not feeling faint?'

'Yes, I'm fine. You are a very good healer, Siv. Thank you.'

Siv bowed his head, but his smile was wide in his swarthy face. 'I am honored to serve. Now if you are ready, we should head off. I'll give you a lift home.'

Her gaze met Earl's and she reached out to him, wanting to touch his skin, feel the realness of him. He didn't stop staring at her and her gaze was just as eager for his. She answered Siv, 'Yes, that would be great. A lift is an excellent idea.'

'Come on then. Let's get you out of here. There is probably enough talent supporting the floor above us.' He put his hand to his mouth. 'Mr Humphrey, are we clear to come up?'

The other council member peeped over the edge. 'We're ready if you are.'

Siv turned back to them. 'We'll be sending in a

team to dispose of the bodies.' His gaze lingered on Pris. 'Is that really the dark witch? The one they all talk about?'

'Yes,' Earl replied before she did.

'Funny. I thought she was younger.'

She frowned. 'Yes, she was. Artificially younger.'

They gazed down at Pris's corpse. Earl shook his head. 'Let's just say her bad deeds caught up to her,' he said with all seriousness.

Siv helped Earl climb out of the basement and then once up, Earl took her hand to lift her out. A vibration tingled her palm. Goddess, he was full of life and power. She couldn't stop her mind from thinking about making love with him. Anticipation made her head swim. He was flesh and blood and real. When she was beside him and focused, a rush of power surrounded her as their energy connected.

Earl looked down at their joined hands and a joyous light filled his eyes. 'Nea,' he said in a soft breath. 'What a thrill to touch you, really touch you.'

Sitting together in Siv's car, the air between them filled with longing and expectation. Her skin yearned for his touch. She had survived death and the best way to celebrate, in her mind, was a night of passion and sexual fulfillment. As she met his gaze she knew he had similar thoughts.

Their time had been short together, but as a reader she had a gift to see what really was and what she could trust. He had more to show her but the essence of him was true. The love and passion she had for him were real. They blossomed inside her. He was real. She was not throwing her life away on a phantom. He knew her body already. She closed her eyes as the strangeness of that situation hit her. There were no surprises for him. For her, though, her fingers ached to explore him, to return the pleasure he had given her, to caress and to love.

In the back seat of the car, she clung to him as he cuddled her. They were on their way back home. It was still hard to take in. Her cheek was pressed against his chest, skin on skin with flesh and blood. This was the Earl of her imagination, the Earl that he had conjured for her to make their relationship more real. His heart beat steadily under her ear and her tears wet the hairs on his chest. Warmth radiated from him. She sighed. Her heart still thumped unsteadily. She'd been close to dying and that seemed surreal. Drew had meant to drain her and kill like Pris had done to Earl—although she knew this she found it hard to believe, to understand. How could anyone consider doing such a thing?

She sighed, realizing it was so. She didn't understand Drew's motivation and she had a hard time even considering someone so dark that they would murder. Intellectually, she knew they existed. The world was riddled with bad humans, bad folk. It was just that she had never experienced it before, not firsthand. The evil in the world hadn't touched her. Perhaps Gregor had sheltered her too much, or perhaps living by the lake had protected her. No, she couldn't blame the old man or her surroundings. There was no one to blame, except Drew and maybe Pris for being lured to darkness, to black magic.

A kiss on the top of her head and she looked up into those hazel eyes haloed in shadow. Earl looked out at her. A sigh escaped. She hardly knew what to think only that where there had been despair there was suddenly hope, and where there had been a future for her without him, it now seemed full of promise.

They arrived home. Earl walked, heading for the

stairs, her hand firmly in his. Inside the house, he knew where to go as he carried her up the stairs and into her room, despite her protests. Kicking the door shut behind him, he placed her on the bed and then looked her up and down. 'A shower I think.'

She couldn't stop looking at him, devouring the sight of him. He'd invoked himself into existence for her. He'd done the unimaginable to save her from that knife.

Looking at herself, she realized the blood on her clothes was not her own. He was covered in blood too, and he had that bit of velvet tied around his middle as no one had found some clothes in all the confusion of their rescue. 'You'll need some clothes,' she said rather lamely.

'I was hoping to go without for a bit …'

She cocked her head, frowning. She was finding it hard to get her thoughts together. She needed to do things, see how Gregor was … but there was Earl in front of her. Her gaze kept coming to him, resting there and then shying away. It was as if she expected him to vanish despite knowing him to be flesh and blood and full of warmth. 'Right then.' She puffed out a breath. 'Um … Jake left some jeans and T-shirts here; they should fit. I'll get those while you have a shower.'

He shook his head, his eyes alight with seduction. He stepped back and nodded to the bathroom.

She found it hard to breathe. This was Earl who'd come into being for her. Forget duty. Forget everything except this man before her. He didn't need clothes. She definitely didn't need clothes. 'What was I thinking?' she said with a laugh.

'I have no idea but come with me.' He held out his hand palm up and then lifted his fingers, inviting her to come along.

She looked down at herself and back at him, a smile breaking out. With a nod, she kicked off her shoes and then peeled off her panties, tossing them in the corner. The remains of her robe came next and the scraps of her bra. All the while her gaze was locked with his. With a tug of her talent, his covering dropped to the floor. She grinned as he blushed. Imagine that—Earl Pressonville blushing. It was delightful.

Her smile grew when she realized he was shy. She shook her head at the wonder of it. The things he had done to her, the joy he had given paled in comparison to this moment. He was alive and a warlock. He might have been a daring phantom, but in real flesh he was hesitant. He was three-dimensional and blinking. She understood that their knowledge of each other was imperfect.

Her body reacted to the scent of him, the physicality of his body and the full interplay of his mind. The phantom had been the essentials of Earl and now he had to navigate his flesh-and-blood life and his relationship to her and others. She sucked in a breath when she comprehended the scale of his adjustment and consequently hers. The power balance between them had shifted. Earl was hesitant and she was sure. She wanted this. She wanted him. It was up to her to take the lead.

'Come on then.' She took his hand and drew him into her tiny bathroom. With her talent, she flicked on the water so that by the time they stepped in under the flow it was hot. Earl shuddered and closed his eyes as the water hit his skin. His expression was half surprise and half adoration.

'Good?' she asked, her gaze eagerly drinking the sight of him in. His hair was now plastered to his head, his eyelashes full with water so that they were even thicker.

'Goddess yes!' He took her hand and kissed her palm, then ran his tongue along her fingers, licking off the water and then sucking the end of each one. Her knees wobbled as her arousal woke. Closing her eyes, she let herself drink in the sensation of his tongue on her skin. It awoke in her the need to use her tongue on him. That body of his was new. No one else had had it. If he was luxuriating in the feel of the shower how would he react to her more tactile exploration? He'd given her the most amazing sexual experience at their first encounter. He'd shredded her reserve and awoken her to new possibilities. Now, she was primed to give even more to him.

Soap suds created a smooth surface in which to run her hands up his body, over his nipples and up along his shoulders as she traced her hands over his biceps down to his hands. His eyes were fixed on her, smoldering and dark. Gently, she guided him to turn around and he acquiesced, his dark gaze never leaving her until he faced the wall. Running her hands up and down his back, she then took in the curve of his taut, rounded buttocks and his strong thighs. Just touching him drew her out of herself and sent shivers of desire into her sex. He turned then and she caught sight of his engorged cock. She knelt and ran her tongue along the tip. Earl shuddered and he locked his knees together. The head went into her mouth and she swirled her tongue around it, tasting him and then sucking him. His hands grabbed her hair and clenched. She opened wider and took him deeper.

'Oh Nea!' His excited words that fell on her ears.

Nea smiled on the inside. It was so good to have someone respond to her, to let her make love to him.

Using her hand, she drew down along his length, keeping the suction on the head.

'Oh please, Nea. Stop! It's divine … I don't want to come yet and I will if you keep that up.'

She eased off but before she stood up, she licked his balls. He did crumble then. Down on his knees, he grabbed her, his lips hot as he sought hers. He crushed her to him, and she loved it and abandoned herself to the embrace.

They kissed—hot, wet and abandoned, then broke off and sucked in a few breaths before diving in again. She reveled in the out-of-control way his mouth tasted hers. Grabbing her hair to tilt her head, he kissed her neck, placing firm pressure on the juncture.

Her blood thumped through her veins. 'Don't stop,' she said and he began to suck and nip at her soft, sensitive flesh. She squirmed as she was driven out of herself. *Goddess! I'm in heaven.*

Together they tumbled to the bathroom floor, then they half crawled along the carpet—hot mouths meeting and parting, then diving for the next piece of flesh. He covered her with his body, his mouth on her neck making her hot and wet. He swapped to the other side, nibbling her ear and then slowly suckling lower until she was a gasping heap of need.

She tried to slide backwards to get to the bed, but they weren't going to make it that far. As soon as she moved back, he latched onto her breast, suckling hard, while beading the other nipple with his fingers. She bucked, shoving her hips upward.

'Not yet, Nea. I'm going to drive you crazy first. Just like you did me.'

He swapped his mouth to her other nipple and she made high-pitched squeaks with each tug on her breast. She was close to coming. He kept up the pressure, his tongue alternating between licking the tip of her nipple and exquisitely suckling her. 'Earl. Oh Goddess!' She breathed deeply. 'You're killing me.'

He lifted his head. 'You won't die from this. You're going to live like you never have before.'

He dove between her breasts, nipping and suckling his way across her belly and further. Anticipation was killing her. Would he lick her? Just the thought had her juices flowing, her breath catching, her mind spinning.

His hot breath whispered across her lower belly, then his tongue tasted her tentatively. A whimper escaped. If he kept this up she was going to jump him and fuck him half to death. Then without warning, he dove in, his mouth cupping her clitoris and his tongue stroking at the same time. She screamed as she came so hard, it took a few minutes for the spasms to fade. Panting, she lay there as Earl held her, then just as she stilled, he dove in again, this time sweeping her labia with his tongue, working his way all over her sex. She cried out. She wanted to get at him but his arm lay over her middle while his mouth exhilarated her. Another climax was building.

'Ahhhh!' she cried out, her tremors leaving her replete. She shook her head. No, she couldn't fade out now. She tried to attack his cock again with her mouth but he held her off.

'No. Not Yet,' he said, his eyes humid with arousal. 'Lean on the bed.'

'Earl, please.'

'I like it when you beg.'

He helped her turn and lay over the edge of the bed. He nudged her knees apart, exposing her. He held her hips and then dove in. She grunted with pure pleasure, feeling abandoned and wanton and full to the brim. His generous cock was bringing every nerve in her body alive.

She was pushing back against him now, begging him to go faster, go harder. He did. The orgasm hit, burst in on her mind. Her voice was ragged from screaming and shouting.

Then he withdrew and stepped back. She flopped down on the bed, face first, head reeling from the heady orgasm.

'Don't fade on me, Nea.'

She flipped over, caught a glimpse of his still hard cock and shivered with anticipation.

'Open your legs,' he said. 'I want to look at you.' Their gazes were locked and she did as he asked. He held her gaze a few moments more and then his eyes shifted. 'Goddess, you're gorgeous. I don't ...' He choked up and tears welled in his eyes. 'I don't deserve you.'

She sat up. 'Earl?'

He stood there, brushing away tears.

'Earl, come to me now. I need you right now.'

His eyelids widened and a laugh escaped him. 'You sure do.' He practically dove onto the bed. 'Be gentle with me,' he said as he leaned in close, breath fanning her face. Real breath from a real man.

Positioning herself, she sucked his bottom lip, nipping it gently. He replied with a groan.

'If I come quickly, it will be your own fault,' he said in mock anger. 'I want this to last for hours."

She laughed out loud. 'If you come too soon, you'll have to start over.'

They were making love for the third time. Exhaustion curled at the edges of Earl's mind and body but he had to keep going, had to have as much of Nea as she could bear.

He could feel her arousal, the lick of flame in her belly, the molten need in her moist cleft. He thought he'd lose that insight now that he was whole and flesh but he hadn't. They still had a connection. Intimacy. If only he'd learned about that before he ...

Dark thoughts of Pris arose. He had to punch them back down. It was done. It was over. This was now.

Her hands feathered along his back, drawing low across the curve of his buttock. The sensation was thrilling. He could sup on that forever, the frisson of her fingers titillating his flesh. He ached to be inside her, but he didn't want to rush. He wanted each time with her to be special. If his experience had taught him anything it was that this could be their only moment. Life and death were full of possibilities. What you had the one minute could disappear forever. He needed to cherish this moment, every moment he had with her. It would always be a gift. Like his gift of life. He owed his redemption to her and he ached to tell her.

Her legs were locked around his. 'Please, please,' she begged him.

He looked down on her heated face, flushed with excitement, and he watched her eyes widen as he slid inside of her. His groan echoed around the room. Nothing could compare to that sensation of being inside her, moist, hot, firm, giving. He slid back and then sunk deeper, capturing her heavy sigh with his mouth, licking her lips, teasing her chin with his teeth.

They moved together, hip to hip, his hand guiding her so they didn't come apart. His tongue captured her nipple and he suckled. Her fingers dug into his neck, holding, urging, begging for more. He enveloped her waist in his hands, lifting, sliding, thrusting. Her cries were music; they set the rhythm, made the pace as he moved in her, with her. And then that moment came when he needed to let go. The pressure was so strong, he couldn't hold it back. It was like the sun rising and setting simultaneously; it was alien and familiar; it was distant and it was now. 'Nea?' And he was gone, blown, sending himself into her and he questioned, wondered, doubted.

She was there, stroking him, kissing him, soothing him with words and touches. It had been real, not a dream. There was wetness between them, exhaustion, sweat, and tears and sighs. Overwhelmed, he found himself with his head on her chest, listening to her heart beat, her soft fingers gently stroking his hair as he wept so suddenly, so inexplicably. He was alive. *I'm alive*, he wanted to say. *Alive because of you.*

And then their minds touched and she knew and felt the same. 'I'm alive because of you too, Earl. I have a life to live because of you. I want … I want to live it with you.'

He drew away. Shame coursed through him. 'I'm not worthy. I don't deserve your life. I wasted mine.'

She put a finger on his lips. Used her thumbs to wipe away his tears. 'I don't care what you've done. This is now. Not then. You've suffered. I tasted your suffering. I was suffering too. I was alone and you were with me, and then I wasn't alone anymore. You spoke to my heart, you filled me up with love and touch and sex, and made it all so extraordinary. I don't care what you've done. I want you in my life.'

'You don't understand … I didn't think clearly. I was obsessed by her. She was deliciously powerful and I couldn't resist.' He thumped his chest. 'I have an essential weakness. I'm unworthy. Your family will see it. Gregor will insist I pay for what I have done.'

'But you saved me. That has to count for something.'

'I couldn't let her use you like she did me or let Drew harm you.'

She hugged him hard, close. 'Earl. Let's not think about it now. Gregor will come home and we will work out a way forward. Please don't talk about un-worthiness.'

'He knew me back then, you know. He won't forget easily.'

Her brows grew together. 'He did? He never mentioned it. But then, he's a cagey old man at the best of times.' She shook her head. 'Never mind. Let's not think about that now. Please. Let's just enjoy the moment.'

They lay together and let the dark of night cover them. Earl let the worldly sounds keep him awake—the sounds of birds and frogs and wind in the trees. He was hearing them with his own ears.

They made love again in the early dawn until Nea was sore and could bear no more. Earl was sore too, but he would bear anything to be with her, inside her, capturing her cries as she came hard, sometimes yelling out her joy. It was so Nea and so right.

The next morning, there was a hail from Hilda before she came up the stairs. They had time to cover themselves with sheets before she opened the door. Her arm was in a cast and her skin had a grayish hue.

'I heard there was a warlock called Earl at the scene,' she said, swallowing before continuing. 'I …' She squinted. 'It is you then?'

Earl glanced at Nea and then back at the older witch. 'Yes, Hilda. It's me.'

Hilda stood still for some time, just looking. 'Re-markable,' she said at last.

'You told me I had to save her and I did.'

'Aye, you did and for her I'm glad … but …' Her cheeks grew pink and she opened and closed her mouth a few times. Then with a frown she spoke. 'You can't be here in the house … or … in bed with Nea.'

Nea stiffened beside him. 'Why not?'

Hilda lowered her eyes. 'Gregor is coming home,' she said in a low voice.

'So?' Nea returned as she sat bolt upright, the sheet pressed to her breast. 'He should be happy Earl saved me.'

Hilda shook her head and let out a low sigh. 'He's grateful you're alive but he is worried about the taint.'

'Taint?' Nea's jaw dropped. 'From Earl?'

Hilda's eyes implored him to help her out.

'Yes, from me.' Earl sat up higher in the bed, his heart thumping. 'From the blood magic.'

'Yes, you have been touched by the blood magic, Nea. You might be free of it, but to knowingly consort with a practitioner could lead to your banishment … and annulment.'

'But that's ridiculous!' Nea turned to him. 'Tell her it's rubbish.'

Earl swallowed and shook his head. 'I can't.'

'What?' Nea said, her voice low.

'I used the blood magic to bring myself back. The blood from Pris called to me. I was desperate and I feel my reasons were just, but in the black-and-white world out there, I'm evil.'

'No,' she said. With her jaw dropping open, she gaped at him and said again, 'No!'

'Earl has to leave the house. Now.' Hilda's tone brooked no argument.

Nea's gaze shifted between them. 'We've only just found each other.' She clutched his hand and held it to her chest. 'This can't be happening.'

Hilda bit her lip, tears glistening in her brown eyes. 'I know this is hard.'

'But he's nowhere to go.' A sob burst out of Nea and tears streaked her cheeks. His heart was torn to shreds at seeing it. The warmth of her spirit had moved him and the warmth of her body had bathed him in love. He was more connected to her than he had been with anyone in his life. Her anguish now was palpable. The future looked dismal indeed.

Hilda closed her eyes and then opened them again. 'I will keep him safe with me.'

Nea's blue eyes flashed. 'And then what? What's going on?'

Hilda brushed her gaze against Earl's form. 'Gregor has had his report. He had an inkling who Earl might be from clues you gave him. Now he's conscious and has been updated on events, he's kicking up a storm.'

Nea chewed her bottom lip. 'He knows about Pris then?'

Hilda nodded.

'So if Earl goes with you, can I see him?'

'Don't make things difficult. The risk for you is being near him. You will share his taint. You could be separated from the coven forever, from Gregor forever.'

Nea's hands twisted in the sheets. 'What? Gregor would cast me out, refuse to see me?'

'Not willingly, but I think he would if it came to it. He cannot bend the rules for his family and keep his place in the coven.'

Nea threw her head back and screamed at the ceiling, one loud cry. He wanted to offer comfort but knew it was pointless. Nea lowered her head and glared at Hilda, a furious calm descending over her. 'You're saying I must choose between Earl and Gregor?'

'I …' Hilda shrugged. 'I hope it will not come to that.'

'But I must see Earl. Please.'

'Not right away. Gregor has called a gathering of the coven here. It will be next week. Earl will have to appear before them if he wants a judgement.'

'I am willing to be judged.' Earl squeezed Nea's hand.

'But a week is so long.' Nea's brow furrowed and her normally bright irises seemed to darken. 'Does this mean it's a trial or something?'

Hilda nodded. 'It's an investigation. Sometimes it is painful. It takes time for folk to gather together, for evidence and witnesses to be assembled. Don't worry —I will look after him.'

Nea nearly tore the sheet in her hand. 'Does Gregor know you'll be doing that?'

Hilda's eyes widened. 'Of course not. Do you think I'm a fool?' She picked up some of Jake's clothes that were on the floor and tossed them at him. 'Put these on. I've got a little cottage outside of town,' she said, directing her words to Nea. 'I used to have a tenant in there. Earl will be safe and hidden. Gregor doesn't know I have it. Not his business really. I'll get Earl some more clothes from the shops after I install him at the cottage.' She stood up straight as if seeing them for the first time. 'Although it doesn't look like he's needed them here—' She smiled knowingly. '— he will need them at my place.'

He made to get out of bed.

'I don't want you to go,' Nea said, grabbing his hand. 'I'll come with you.'

'Nea ...'

'Please,' she said. 'Don't leave me behind.'

He brushed her tousled hair back from her wide set eyes. 'It will be all right. Trust me and let the coven judge me. If I'm found to be safe ... untainted then we can be together, free and clear.'

'I ... I don't trust Gregor to be fair.'

A scoff from behind her. 'Gregor doesn't get to make the decision alone. Earl's judgement will be fair. But if you do the wrong thing now it could go bad for you as well. Earl needs to keep out of Gregor's way until the gathering convenes. There's no telling what that pig-headed mule will do.' Hilda cast a look at Earl. 'It seems you're more of a problem in the flesh than you were as a phantom, and he has figured out who you really are. Not that I know who you are—before my time and all that, aye. But now the stupid doctor has gone and told him he can come home as long as he takes it easy, there's no stopping him.'

'I will visit him, explain how it is,' Nea said, making to get out of bed.

Hilda shook her head. 'No you won't. It's too late anyhow. He's likely already on his way. Don't make things tougher than they are. If you do that, then Gregor will come home and he'll discover that I've sheltered Earl. Then we'll all be in a pickle.'

'I wouldn't tell him.'

'Yes, but Gregor knows you and knows me and even though being a reader isn't his major talent, I bet he could weasel Earl's whereabouts out of you before you blinked.'

Nea stilled and thought it through. 'You'd risk your relationship with Gregor for us?'

Hilda shrugged. 'I hope I'm not risking anything. I am my own woman, after all, and he knows that and so far has respected it. Yet, I want to keep the odds in my favor. What a man doesn't know and all that. It's not that I'll keep it from him but I'll let him know in my own way and my own time. You see, I'm helping Earl, but I'm also ensuring that he sticks around for the judgement. No one will have to go on the hunt for him.'

'I already said I wanted to be judged,' Earl said rather hotly.

Nea looked between them. 'She's not criticizing you. She's strategizing so she can deal with Gregor and come out unscathed. But I still …'

He squeezed Nea's hand. 'It will be all right. We can hail each other.'

They looked at Hilda. 'Best not,' she said. 'Gregor is a smart one and I don't want him to know. Not yet. Not until the issue of you is dealt with.'

Nea opened her mouth to argue but Hilda put up her hand. 'Don't. I've had enough of your grandfather and I don't need the same from you. Royston's stubborn to the bone marrow. Why, he had the nerve to order *me* to stay in bed. I'm quite all right. Nothing a few good dosings won't fix.' She turned to leave the room. 'Get dressed. I'll be downstairs.'

As she turned to leave, she wavered and grabbed the doorjamb for support, belying her pronouncement that she was doing all right. 'Mmm … maybe you should be quick about that. We need to be well gone before Gregor gets here and I need to lie down.' She put a hand to her head. 'Soon, in fact.'

CHAPTER ELEVEN

Nea was up and dressed by the time the car arrived with Gregor. Humphrey drove. He nodded to her as he got out and then opened the passenger door.

Gregor heaved himself out and then wavered as he stood. For support, he held onto the roof of the car and the door. Humphrey stayed out of his way. A cloud of gloom hung over her grandfather's head.

She stood at the top of the stairs. *Like that, was it? Black mood, Gregor.* She backed down the hallway, not being able to look as her stubborn grandfather made his way up the stairs without assistance.

It wasn't his anger so much as the sight of him brought so low. He'd been attacked in his own house. He was the head of the coven, supposedly the strongest of them all, the protector and defender. He was shamed, and that made him furious with himself and the world in general.

It seemed to take an age before he loomed in the doorway. He stood there, his head bandaged, bruising around his eye. He beckoned to her and she surged forward to wrap her arms around his girth. Out of nowhere tears came and she sobbed while he held her. Then he patted her on the shoulder when her tears slowed. She loved Gregor more than life itself and she could no more hurt him than cut out her own heart. But then she thought of Earl and how much she loved him, needed him, and how connected in spirit they were. She swallowed a lump just thinking about having to choose between the two men.

'Help me to sit down, will you?' And putting his weight on her shoulders, he ambled over to his chair and plonked himself down. He sighed and then adjusted himself, leaning against the head rest. 'It's good to see you, Nea.' He patted her hand, signaling that he didn't need her assistance anymore. Yet she knew he wasn't done.

'A cuppa then?' she asked, a small smile playing around her mouth.

'Oh yes please. I've put the kettle on.' Gregor gave her an answering smile and then winced, revealing that he really was not as hale as he was trying to make out. It wouldn't surprise her if he hadn't related all his symptoms and injuries to the doctors.

As she walked into the kitchen, she heard the kettle boiling away. Gregor using his talent for mundane things again. She didn't think she'd get used to it, but it was his house. She grabbed a tissue to blow her nose and then washed her hands before making the tea. As she went through the process of setting the cups, something she'd done hundreds, maybe thousands of times before, she knew things were different. He was home but things weren't going to get back to normal. They'd passed through a crisis and nothing would be the same. They both knew it, but accepting it was going to take some working out.

For her, things had changed irrevocably. Part of her rebelled at the thought. She didn't want their life to alter. She didn't want to leave Gregor or modify their domestic situation. Yet she knew things were already different. Gregor had a relationship with Hilda, although he'd said nothing about it. It was there. She'd heard them making love, knew him to be lonely, knew beyond doubt that Hilda loved him. Hilda was no pushover, thank the Goddess, so the next little while was going to be interesting.

She suspected there would be a relationship, a permanent one. That did not necessarily mean that she could not be part of that. Her love for Gregor and his for her would not falter—change and adapt, maybe. But what if she went against Gregor's wishes? What if she left with Earl? What if they ran away before the judgement? Her hands shook with the thought. Her heart beat so hard she thought it would choke her and a knot of fear twisted in her gut. Not only would they be pursued and dealt with like blood magic fiends, but he would have to disown her. What if they didn't run away but Earl was judged to be a dark one and either killed or annulled and banished? Next week. Just so soon as next week with her constrained from contacting him directly.

Earl was in her life. She wanted him there, but there were hurdles. Gregor had to approve, and there was a history there. Earl was so caught up in guilt that he needed a judgement to move forward. Could she bear that? Could she bear to know what he had done? Could she bear to know the details of how he came to be a not-dead spirit at the hands of Pris, the dark witch of the north? And his rebirth? Even she knew it involved blood magic. He'd taken back what was his, but was that morally right? Would that act forever taint him?

Dark thoughts flew at her, increasing her uncertainty about the future, about her life. What about

Drew? Where had he gone? Was he part of this new movement that worked to extend the practice of the dark arts, to make folks stand out from humans? It seemed likely. Would they be called on to become battle mages?

As she poured the water she let out a sigh. That was too much speculation. She needed to bring herself back to now, to what was in front of her, to what was within her control, her span of influence, reminding herself that her love for Earl was real, ripened from a deep spiritual connection and helped along by a very large dose of sex.

Assembling the tea things on the tray, she searched for some biscuits to put on the plate. Gregor would notice the lack of them. He needed routine and the taste of home to settle his mind, to soothe his hurt. He and Hilda had been attacked here. His wards had been breached, his power mocked. There was a lot he had to deal with and she wanted to ease his way as best she could. She had to admit she wanted to deflect any potential anger against Earl too. So she would keep hold of her tongue. For now, at least.

As she glanced at the assembled tea things, she realized she'd used Bess's tea service. She blinked in surprise. The teapot was delicate in her hands as she poured and then passed over some honey biscuits that Hilda had made.

Gregor noticed. His hand stilled as he took the cup, and he sent her a questioning look.

She shrugged. 'I don't know why I used it.'

He harrumphed. 'Don't worry about it. Appropriate. It's like it invokes her presence and that always soothes me. Ah Bess ... I came close to joining her. Did you know that?'

She swallowed and wiped at a tear borne from the

twist of emotion in his words, that premonition of loss. 'No. I didn't.'

As she watched his face, she saw the sag in his cheek and the twinkle disappear from his eyes. 'I have failed you all,' he said in a voice that had hit emotional rock bottom.

She sucked in a gentle breath, trying to think of a way to comfort him. 'Drew is very powerful, Grandpa. He killed the dark witch and stole power from another warlock. He's obviously been hiding his talent and strength. He took you by surprise is all.'

He lowered his gaze to the cup. 'I'm less than I was, Nea. Bess died and I was made less. I'm old, too, and that makes me less. I failed to protect my own and that unravels me.'

'No, don't think that. You're what you were. Your power is undiminished. It's just that Drew had more and he stole what he got. He used dark magic.'

'That may be so, but I see my days are numbered.'

She moved to sit on the floor by his knee. 'Oh Grandpa. Don't say that. You are our leader.'

His shoulder's squared and he straightened his posture. 'Yes, I'm your leader.' He looked down at her, and she saw the shift in him as his gaze intensified. 'I want you to stay away from Earl Pressonville.'

She jerked. The bastard had played her, she was sure. 'But Grandpa ...'

'If you love and respect me you'll do as I say.'

Definitely, he was using the emotional bludgeon. She knew it but couldn't budge from under it. With tears in her eyes, she nodded. Until Gregor had his gathering and performed the judgement she'd abide by his wishes. No sneaking out and visiting Earl. She'd have to communicate the old-fashioned way, slyly, with messages through a third party—Hilda.

A week later and Gregor summoned her to the gathering. While looking in the mirror, Nea tidied her hair, stalling so her confused feelings would settle and so that she could face her grandfather calmly. Inwardly, she was happy that he was whole, that the attack had not injured him permanently, but the tremor of passion she could feel in the air told her that he remained angry. For him to still be simmering at this time was not a good sign. It was time to face it.

She turned to the door of her room and hesitated. Earl had told her he'd had a past and she'd accepted that. Knew that he had suffered the unbearable and come out whole. She had to admire him for that, for the strength of spirit that had turned sorrow into hope and error into truth. She knew he'd been wild in his earlier days and had repented, had those rough edges worn away.

Sighing long, she grabbed the door handle and headed down the stairs. It was all right for her. She hadn't known Earl then, nearly thirty odd years ago now. But Gregor had. He remembered what had happened, and forgiveness was not his strong point.

Her heart skipped a beat as her foot hit the ground floor. She hadn't seen Earl since Hilda had taken him to stay in her little cottage on the edge of town. Closing her eyes, she tried to calm her lurching heartbeat. Excitement at seeing her lover had to be controlled. All would be watching them.

Despite her earlier bravado, Hilda had kept quiet about harboring Earl so as to not anger Gregor. He was the leader of the coven and she was in love with him. Sheltering Earl secretly was all she was prepared to do and she would risk nothing more. She would not advocate for him.

She had witnessed the first meeting between Hilda and her grandfather after Gregor had returned home from the hospital. Their relationship had been strained and the good will between them was tenuous. Mostly it was Gregor being so wounded for not protecting the women in his life. He couldn't forgive himself. He was gruff when speaking to Hilda, which Nea suspected was to keep the other woman at a distance. Hilda had given her a dark look and a slight shake of the head.

Nea couldn't help reading her. The older witch was hurting, yet there was nothing either of them could do to shift the old man's view. He had to come to accept the situation himself. However, if he found out that Hilda had sheltered Earl, it would make matters worse. If he knew Hilda had helped them communicate, it would be worse still.

Another hail came from Gregor, one with a hint of impatience. She glanced at her reflection in the hall mirror and grimaced. Time to face it. Tears stung her eyes then when she thought that this might be the last time she would see her new found love. Her grandfather was likely to send her away when they did the judgement. Not only because of Earl but because of the harm that was nearly done to her and what had been done to them all. He'd want to protect her whether she wanted that protection or not. Her stomach flip-flopped. She feared she would have to choose between the men she loved and feared she could not.

Worst of all, Drew had definitely escaped. No one in the coven had found a trace of him, and they'd been looking hard. Somehow he'd lived through Earl's deathblow. He'd climbed to his feet, shaken off the hex and walked away in the bare seconds it took Humphrey, Siv and the other councillors to arrive. The coven was all abuzz about it. Reports had been sent to Sydney and other covens in Queensland and overseas. Yet no reports of Drew had surfaced. That worried everyone. She didn't need to be a reader to know that. She could almost taste the fear.

Uprisings, like those that had been happening in Europe, could happen here. Australia, the protected, distant backwater was likely to be thrust into the forefront of a magical battle for supremacy. Human and folk were not going to be spared.

With a wipe at her tears and a large intake of breath, she opened the door to the large living room that served as a council chamber. A number of councillors stood around, glancing nervously at each other. The air was tense, power was hidden away, and when she faced them all, eyes were cast down. Her gaze fell on Gregor sitting in his customary armchair. She almost grinned at seeing him there like his old self, brimming with power and authority. A stern look from him checked her desire to throw her arms around his neck and weep with the joy of it.

'Took you long enough,' Gregor said with a grunt and a lift of his head.

'I'm sorry. I'm glad to see you, too.' She wanted to call him Grandpa just to niggle at the hard, glowering façade he wore, but that wouldn't help his feelings of unworthiness.

'Don't try to bamboozle me, Bethanea Royston. You've been consorting with a dark one and that's a serious crime for one of the coven, my granddaughter or no.'

'A dark one? What are you talking about? I went out with Drew at your instigation.'

'I'm not talking about Drew Penderton. I'm

talking about Earl Pressonville, the dark one you've had in your bed.'

She bristled at the anger and the accusation in his voice. She tried catching Hilda's eye but the witch, who stood to the right of Gregor, kept her gaze on the floor. What would Gregor say about his lover hiding the said dark one in her cottage?

Instead of responding, she sucked in a breath and tossed her head back, fixing Gregor with her gaze, a trick he often did to others. 'Earl Pressonville is not a dark one. Nor was he ever one, not truly. He dabbled, yes. He did things he has atoned for. You can't punish him forever.'

'What do you know but what he's told you? He has warped your mind with sex, with his dark arts.'

'I wasn't aware that sex was a dark art,' she threw back at him.

There was a murmur amongst the gathered council.

'I never took you for a smart ass, Nea. This is serious. Very serious. You will have to be examined.'

She blinked. 'Me? Examined?'

'Yes, three councillors will probe you to ensure you haven't been touched by the dark. There will be pain.' His white brows lowered over his piercing blue eyes.

She didn't like that one bit. 'I am not touched by the dark and neither is Earl. Go ahead. Examine me.'

He lifted his head. 'If that's the case, why isn't he here defending himself, defending you?'

There was movement behind her, but she kept her gaze steady on her grandfather, dismayed by the lack of warmth she could read in him. Her gaze sought Hilda's again but the woman was looking past her, her jaw dropping.

'I am here to defend myself. Nea has nothing to answer for.'

She closed her eyes, his voice tingling against her skin. It was bliss to hear him speak. His real voice resonated within her soul. But he wasn't meant to come. They'd agreed.

She swung around. 'You aren't meant to be here.' She let that slip. In their time apart, she had urged him to stay away from the judgement, from Gregor's wrath. He hadn't listened to her pleadings. He had ignored her notes.

Earl was dressed in jeans, with a white T-shirt and grey sweater. She was amazed how ordinary clothes suited him. How he'd created that body was still a mystery to her, but she loved every inch of it. He assured her that it was himself, as he used to be.

It was so hard not to throw herself into his arms at that moment. She clenched her hands until her fingernails imprinted in her palm. It was essential to remain composed.

Earl's eyes left Gregor, who'd stiffened and sat up straighter in his chair, and then settled on her. The light from the window emphasized the green flecks in his hazel eyes and then he turned his head slightly, making his irises look dark again. 'I couldn't stay away. Not when you were in danger. I can defend myself. I'm ready to face judgement.' To Gregor and the assembled council, he said, 'Nea was not exposed to the dark through me. If you have another reader in your midst, you will find that. There is no need to examine her. That's too drastic. She has done nothing to warrant that. Me, on the other hand? I'm ready to face an examination. I want you to know it all. I want to repent of my wrongdoings and face your judgement.'

Gregor harrumphed, then lifted his head to stare

at Earl, his blue eyes bright. He cupped his chin with his hand, the fingers brushing the bandage that hid his stitches. 'You look the same as you did then,' he said quietly, and she could tell her grandfather was remembering the past. 'It's hard to believe that you're here now. You want us to believe you're without taint, that you shouldn't be punished for what you did all those years ago?'

'I don't expect you to forgive, Gregor. That was never in your nature. But I do expect you to give me a chance to redeem myself. I expect you to provide me with a path to forgiveness so I can be with your granddaughter, Bethanea.'

Gregor's hand clenched the arm of his chair. Then he lifted it and slapped it down hard. 'Never.'

'Grandpa, please. I don't know what happened when you were younger. I don't know the exact details what Earl did before Pris ended him, but I'm a reader. You've trusted me before. I'm telling you he has suffered greatly. He has, over time, repented and sorrowed for his past mistakes. You should also take into account that he saved me, saved me from certain death. I could be like he was—alive but not dead, or just plain dead. Others have died at the dark witch's hands. Earl cannot explain why he lived when others didn't.'

She took a step forward, moving her gaze from Gregor to Earl. 'But there must be a reason, something special about him for that to happen. When I first encountered him, there was nothing but misery and suffering. He existed in a place without light and hope, unable to die and unable to live. He said my light woke him up, Grandpa.' Tears coursed down her cheeks. 'He was drawn to me, to my lightness. That lightness comes from you. Your blood runs through me. Please don't turn your back on him, on justice—be open to the possibilities of what he represents.

'He took back the power and life that Pris stole from him. He didn't strike the blow. It wasn't him. It was Drew who lusted for that power. It was only when my life was in danger did he reform himself, taking back what was stolen. It's remarkable. It's not evil or dark.'

'Nea.' Gregor's voice was low. 'Enough.'

'No, I can see it's not enough. If you can't be impartial, if you can't … can't do that … then let someone else do it.'

'Nea,' he warned.

'Our essences have touched. I have chosen him to be my life mate. If you separate us you might as well kill me.'

Gregor scoffed. 'I never took you for fanciful. Always the practical one.'

'I speak the truth as I understand it.'

He looked her up and down and his gaze flicked to Earl. 'Enough said now. We will decide later.'

'No, it's not enough. Earl is a creator, a conjurer. His talent is creating illusion. I know you've kept this threat of the rise of the dark ones away from me, but you can't hide it forever. Earl will be useful as a battle mage. There are so few of us with the ability to fight.' Nea stepped closer to her grandfather, his eyes not leaving her, and she knelt by his knee as she used to do as a child. She dared not read him, dared not see if her words were having an effect. 'Please have mercy, Grandpa. Please.'

Gregor placed his hand on her head as Nea laid her cheek against his knee. While she had not read him, there had been a subtle shift in the tension in his body. The simmering rage seemed to have quietened, although he was by no means at peace.

Earl stood in the centre of the room, calm, his hands clasped in front of him. Gregor patted her head, stroked her like he did the cat in the evenings. He lifted his head and addressed Earl. 'So you want to be examined?'

Earl lifted his chin higher, not breaking eye contact. 'Yes. The sooner the better.'

'I understand.'

Nea blinked as she looked around the room. Earl had no one here to vouch for him. She could not. She was too involved. Yet, she had to trust that the judgement would be fair. Gregor could not disregard her words, her earnest defense of her lover.

'You have the right to choose your examiners,' Gregor said. 'Who do you want?'

Earl's shoulders sagged. She reached out tentatively with her talent. He was relieved that he'd gotten that far. Beneath, there was a wealth of emotions riding him. He caught her gaze and nodded. She drew back her talent.

Earl's gaze travelled around the room. 'Hilda Ngati,' he said when he looked to the right of Gregor. He continued to take in the people in the room. To the left, he paused and said, 'Humphrey Basewater.' He looked around him casually and shrugged. Then, meeting Gregor's bright gaze, he added, 'And you, Gregor Royston.'

Gregor jerked in surprise. 'Me? But ...'

She nearly fainted. Gregor was not someone she thought he would choose.

'You were there with me in my youth. You hated me then and you hate me now, I know ... but I trust in your sense of right. I know you will judge me fairly. I wouldn't want to be with your granddaughter if I was not worthy of her.'

The council members started whispering. She

was on her feet. 'No! You can't do that.' She whirled. 'Refuse him, Grandpa, please.'

'I can't,' he said, shaking his head. 'I am charged with a duty I must fulfill.'

She lunged at Earl and wrapped her arms around him. 'I'm afraid. I'm afraid this will be the last time I hold you.'

He took her by the shoulders and edged her away from him. 'I'm not afraid. You gave me something that I'll cherish beyond the grave. We had something special and no matter what happens, that can't be taken away.'

'No, no. Don't say that.' Tears tracked down her cheeks and she was too distraught to wipe them away or be ashamed as her nose ran too.

'Bethanea, you must leave us now. We will begin.'

At Gregor's word, those not on the council had to leave the room. She was led out. In the hall, she knew she couldn't be in the house either. She had to leave, had to find a way to distance herself. She was a reader. She'd feel Earl's pain and she knew the examination would hurt him.

Around the back of the house, she gazed out onto the lake. The day was bright but slightly windy. The boat rocked against the pier. It was the family launch. She'd take it out for a cruise.

Hastily checking that all was in order—petrol, flares, life jacket, water, snacks already stacked in the cupboard—she turned the engine over and idled it while she slipped the mooring.

CHAPTER TWELVE

Earl watched as the room emptied, leaving him alone with his three examiners. Hilda brought him a chair and gestured for him to take a seat. He kept his gaze locked with Gregor's. He'd taken a risk. There was history between them. For him the memories were fresh, but with Gregor he could tell they'd fallen into the cracks and hardened like mud in the old warlock's mind.

Breaking eye contact, he took a seat. It was wood and its hard edges dug into his skin. It was uncomfortable, and it was marvelous. He had a real, flesh body. Not an imaginary one, not one he'd fashioned out of his talent so he could interact with Nea. A real body that had nerves and hormones and emotions, and all of them were churning inside. He couldn't stop or control it. It was painful and it was exhilarating. He was alive. The outcome of this examination could change all that. And still he wouldn't change a thing. He wouldn't be who he was if he hadn't suffered, if Nea's presence hadn't touched him, if he hadn't loved her and been loved in return. While he wanted his life to continue and to share it with Nea, he knew that if he died, if his life was suddenly over, he'd be fulfilled, knowing he had been worthy of her love and also redeemed by saving her.

Hilda stood in front of him. 'It has been decided that I will lead this examination. Earl Pressonville, do you consent?'

'I do.'

'Then open to me.'

He swallowed and his palms grew sweaty. 'Yes.' He closed his eyes, dropped all his barriers and took a breath. A wedge slammed into him. He gripped his seat to stop himself from falling. The black wedge pushed further, harder, splitting his mind until he screamed. He could hear those screams in his ears; he could hear them in his memories. They had been there—at the moment of his ending thirty years ago.

The pain, the despair rose up and was examined. Pris, young then, rutting with him, his blood trailing down his torso as she took from him, grinding her mound on his erection, tendrils of his power snaking out of him as she devoured his essence. He'd barely understood the ritual as the words of her chant had encircled him.

The wedge drove further in, delving deeper back in time to when he'd first met the young, dark witch. He had been smitten by her then—the elegant curve of her neck, her long, luxuriant dark hair that cascaded in waves down her back. He'd not been the only one to lust after her physically. Then there was the hard wall of power she projected. You knew it was there, but you couldn't get a taste of it, just the sense that there was something earth-shattering inside of her.

In those days, Pris hadn't lived amongst them. She'd visited from time to time. Glimpses of her were occasional. It was hard to believe she'd been so young when she first appeared among them. One day he'd seen her full with child. He'd been stunned. She didn't seem the type to want to breed. She was so young, so beautiful and powerful—why would she want to sully her life with a child? He was young and mating, and bringing children into the world was alien to his view of life.

That had been their first real encounter. 'You're spying on me,' she'd accused him.

'No, not at all. Our meeting is entirely coincidental.'

'Forget you saw me. Tell anyone and I'll know.' Then, with a wave of her hand and a harsh whisper, she'd hexed him. He'd been doubled up in agony for nearly a day and then had a nasty rash that lasted two weeks, two weeks of weeping sores and being bedridden, and he too proud to seek a healer to ameliorate the curse.

Then she went away and he didn't see her again until a few years later. He'd heard rumors of her, a supposed dark witch. His friend Maxim invited him to the old house. Pris's place. It was there that he saw her, dressed in her velvet robes of black or crimson, depending on her mood. There he saw her entice the young men. Human, warlock—she cared not.

He had wanted her. The grace with which she moved, the smooth white of her hand as she caressed a cheek or ruffled hair was so enticing. It was a spell. The way she liked them to watch while she took her favorite, rode him, bringing them both to climax.

It was her experimentation with darkness, he thought. Was he responding to a question? Yes, perhaps her descent into darkness. He didn't know. He was on the outer. He looked on, mesmerized as any young man would be when exposed to public sex for the first time.

He knew humans watched porn, but nothing

could match what he saw. Maybe there was a spell on them. He was too ignorant to tell—too transfixed by her beauty and her daring to notice.

How many were there? The question was asked. There were nine other males. Three humans, all muscles and leather, a few tattoos on chests or backs. The rest were warlocks. Two were from outside the coven. He'd only ever seen them in Pris's presence. The others were from the coven.

Who were they?

Me, Charlie Depson, Wei Chung and Maxim Beauchamp.

Things went along like that for months and months. He was never chosen to be the one she mated with. Charlie told him he'd rutted with her during the week. That he slept in her bed. He said, too, that she was into kink. That she tied him up, beat him and then rutted him senseless. He'd been afraid. It had hurt but it was the best thing ever.

Earl had been angry with him. Charlie had had what he wanted. He wanted to be noticed. He wanted to be her special man, her special experience. Then one day, it happened.

He shivered at the memory. They came to her place at the usual time. He came in last and locked the door behind him. Charlie was trussed to a pole in the centre of the room. He rocked back on his heels. Welts stood out on Charlie's naked flesh, red cuts leaking blood against his pale flesh. His eyes were blackened and swollen shut.

He had trembled at the sight of him there. He knew then that this was no erotic adventure—this was punishment. He knew, also, that he might be drawn into that. He suspected Charlie was not meant to tell him what went on in the dark witch's bed.

He remembered her hex about seeing her pregnant. He knew she had the power to know if Charlie spoke of it. Charlie had been full of himself, wanting to rub it in that Earl was on the outside. It was no secret why he kept coming back week after week. He wanted to be the one. He had climaxed time and time again with visions of Pris in his mind as he dealt with himself by hand.

'You see one who has transgressed. One who has injured me,' Pris hissed at her audience of followers, her face full of rage.

Her dark gaze flicked from face to face. He thought her gaze lingered on him, but he couldn't tell for certain. His heart thumped in his chest. He was guilty. Charlie had spoken to him. Earl had listened and had trespassed.

'Will anyone speak in his defense?'

There were whispers, but no one volunteered. Earl could not speak. Charlie had spoken to him. How could he defend the other warlock? It would bring him her wrath.

'Will anyone damn him with their words?'

Her eyes were on Earl then, and he knew that she knew what had happened. He broke eye contact and struggled. Charlie was his friend. Yes, the young warlock had meant to wound him, but he understood. Pris was the prize. Charlie wanted Earl's envy.

Earl had looked up and Pris was right in front of him. Her light perfume surrounded him. Her lush mouth was in a pout. 'Surely you know of what I speak?' Pris said.

Earl nodded. Her hand reached out and took his limp one. 'Come forward, Earl Pressonville.'

She drew him along with her, past where Charlie whimpered from pain and fear. 'Tell me, Earl,' she said, drawing her fingers through his hair, twisting the curling ends between her forefinger and thumb. 'What did Charlie do?'

He swallowed around the lump in his throat. Her touch was driving him wild. His erection hurt so much as it pressed against his zip. His thoughts swirled. Images of her kissing him, touching him made concentrating hard. 'He spoke of forbidden things. He spoke of being with you when he swore he would not.' He blinked. 'He betrayed you.'

Her face was composed and she nodded. Her dark eyes moved from Earl to Charlie. 'Yes, my beautiful Charlie betrayed me. Betrayed my love.'

Earl's gaze was fixed to her face, seeing the light flush high in her cheeks, the dark lashes casting a shadow when she lowered them. 'And what must his penalty be?'

Earl blinked then, tried to pull away, but he was held firm in her grip, not by a physical grip, but a mental one. Words came out of his mouth. 'He must die.'

He tried to fight against what he'd said, to put in a counter argument, to deny it, but he could not. They were not his words. He was in thrall. He didn't know whether that was his own weakness or her power. He couldn't tell.

Her followers fell to their knees, stripped off their clothes. Earl sat beside her fully dressed, unable to move. Pris picked up her sacred blade and stood. She shrugged off her robe and stood in her beauty, her breasts full with dark nipples, her hips flaring to a round bottom with creamy, unblemished skin, her shapely legs stepping close to beaten and trussed warlock who began to cry, a soft weeping. Words came out of his mouth but they made no sense.

Pris chanted now, her voice filling the room. The others swayed back and forth in time, drawn into her magic. Earl sat immobilized as the knife struck. Blood spurted from Charlie's jugular, covering Pris's breasts with crimson. Drawing a finger along her skin, she licked the blood. 'Drink in, all of you.'

It was then Earl perceived the energy that flowed along with the blood. It was drawn in by the others, drawn in by Pris. 'Earl,' she called in a dark, deep voice. 'Come here to me.'

Suddenly free, he stood up and stumbled over to her. She used the bloodied blade to cut away his clothes. His erection was still there and it spilled into her bloodied hands. The energy from Charlie was less now as he died, but it sunk into him as her hands covered his cock in blood. His skin tingled and the power surging into him was mind-shatteringly invigorating. It was one small part that leaked into him. Pris drew the rest in. He was in awe at how she could do that. This was blood magic!

Nea distanced herself from her home, then stopped the engine and let down the anchor. The opposite shore was not too far away and here she couldn't sense the emanations coming from her home or from Earl's pain. She was out of hailing distance too. Out of the way of temptation of listening in or getting an update on proceedings.

Normally the soft bounce of the boat would have soothed her and the light playing on the water given her delight. Not today. She leant against the rail, her heart tearing itself into pieces. What was she going to do? How would she deal with the outcome? What if they killed Earl accidentally or annulled and banished him? What would she do? Gregor had been her life. Could she abandon him and go away with Earl, never to communicate again?

Looking down, she realized she was gripping the rail so hard that her skin had gone white. Carefully, she let go, peeling stiff fingers off. Tears were hastily wiped away. The boat shuddered and she caught a glimpse of something on the bow. *What was that?*

Three warlocks died. Their bodies found. How did they die? The question was from Gregor and came like a hammer in his mind.

The men who came to Pris's changed over time. Maxim stopped coming, after rutting with Pris for a month. Charles was killed in front of us. Wei lasted two months before he stopped coming.

You were not involved in their deaths? Gregor continued to question.

Pain stabbed into him. Earl writhed. No. Except for Charles, I didn't know they were dead. They just stopped coming.

What about Pris? That question was softer.

She grew more powerful. We were together once only. It was a blur of sex and pain. She didn't parade me like she had the others, but her desires grew more strange.

You participated in more murders? The impenetrable wall could only be Gregor.

Only my own, Earl replied.

The memory then came hurtling out of the dark recesses of his mind. He'd been tied, the ropes cutting into him as he'd fought her ministrations. Then the knife had slit across his chest at the moment of release. He'd been too far in the moment to even register it. Then she'd licked at his blood and he'd known that she'd done it. Ended him.

❁

Foreboding swept up Nea's spine and made her hands tingle. She was no longer alone on the boat. She took a step and then stilled. Drew Penderton strode into her line of sight. *How did he get here? Oh no, he's back to finish me off.*

As if he read her thought, he held out his hand and then clenched his fingers. She was seized and then drawn forward. Her power split around her, seeking traction against the ship rails and finding none.

'So you're alone. How nice for me,' Drew said as she neared. Her resistance had slowed the pull but not stopped it. 'I've not forgotten what you owe me.'

A calmness enveloped her. With a sudden decision, she stopped resisting his pull and put power in her forward movement.

Surprised, his eyes widened, just as her head struck him. Unprepared, he reeled backwards. 'Fuck. That hurt, bitch!'

Prepared, she rolled towards the cabin and then climbed to her feet. Drew might be powerful, but he wanted something from her. Her power, certainly, but something more. Submission maybe. *A witness to his supreme talent?*

The battle mage exercises came in handy. She was no match for him, but she could resist and she could attack if she was smart about it. Now wasn't the time to get herself killed. She had Earl, didn't she? What if she lived and Earl was banished? What if she died and he lived on without her? *It can't end like that.*

Drew struck out at her. She flew backwards and

landed badly, flipping over the rail and ended up dangling over the side of the boat. She swung her legs up and climbed back on board. If only she hadn't anchored. The drift would have brought her close to shore. She could have swum for it. *Swim for it? With a dark mage trying to kill you? Hardly!*

'Come on, Nea. Give it up. Come willingly and I could be merciful.'

'You, merciful? You want to kill me and take my essence. How is that merciful?'

His dark eyes watched her closely. 'I could make it pleasurable for you. I could let your boyfriend live.'

Her eyes widened but she kept quiet. 'I'm sorry, but I'm not going to go meekly to slaughter. I'm a Royston and we're a stubborn breed. I'm fighting you with the last drop of my life force. There won't be much left for you to take.'

His mouth twitched. Not quite a smile. 'Now you're teasing me. You know I like it when people squirm.'

She lifted her eyebrow and then whacked him one with a body blow, one that she had been building slowly while he was distracted. Declan Mallory's book was awfully good.

Drew hadn't expected a show of power. He doubled over and landed on his butt. The red in his face let her know she'd winded him. It wasn't a killing blow. She didn't think she could end him, but she wasn't going easily.

'Bitch. You're gonna pay for that.'

Darkness descended, suffocating darkness. The metal of the deck pressed against her cheek. The air was like liquid and she couldn't breathe. She had to find a way to fight this attack. Her body would shut down soon. Breathe. Breathe. She had no breath.

Earl's pain levels rose as the examiners delved deeper, testing the truth of Earl's memories. His heart fluttered. He was conscious that his hair was wet with sweat. The sounds of breathing reached his ears, and the shape of the furniture and the walls took form around him. And then the minds and the banked power of the witch and the two warlocks examining him withdrew. They stepped back, their heads lowered.

He sat up and looked at them, not quite believing the examination was over. Now it was time for the judgement.

'He didn't kill anyone,' Hilda said.

'He's guilty of not reporting a crime,' Gregor added with anger lacing his words.

'It isn't clear to me that he's guilty,' Humphrey said. 'There was a spell; she held him bound.'

'He's guilty of nothing more than being young and gullible.' This was Hilda. 'He has suffered,' she added, her voice clogged with emotion. Was that pity for him in her tone, in her tear-stained face?

'He has suffered,' the other two agreed.

Earl's ears pricked up. Gregor had spoken along with Humphrey.

'He has atoned for the mistakes he made,' the older witch said, her voice rising, filled with conviction.

'Agreed,' said Humphrey readily.

Gregor's eyebrows lowered and he shook his head. The other two turned to face him. 'Gregor, what is your judgement?'

'There was much in the telling. I remember those young warlocks, now lost to us. He remembers being held in thrall, in Pris's power. Could his version of events be true?'

Humphrey spoke. 'I tested the veracity of his memory and I could sense no lie, no interference.'

'Yes,' Hilda said. 'There was no hedging. It's an honest recall. He revealed all, more than he needed to. He revealed the bad along with the good in himself.'

Gregor rubbed his chin and shook his head. 'He was a fool.'

Earl lifted his eyes, his headache lessening somewhat now that the psychic pressure had been removed. He had been drained in the telling, his own talent consumed. Wryly, he thought that he was vulnerable now. If these folk wanted to nullify his power or end him, then he was prepped and ready. Nothing he did could stop them. He'd be lost to Nea forever. Dismay threatened to overwhelm him. The wetness of tears trailed down to drip from his chin. Thoughts of Nea rose in his mind.

As if they suddenly noticed his presence they all turned to him. Humphrey's expression was somber. 'Gregor, you have yet to voice your judgement. How do you find Earl Pressonville? Do you find he is free of the taint of blood magic?'

'Not entirely free,' Gregor said slowly, his bright blue eyes fixed on Earl.

Hilda drew in a breath. 'Do you find him guilty of murder?' she asked.

'No, I do not find him guilty of murder. Stupidity yes, but I tasted the dark witch's power on him. He was powerless in her thrall and afraid too. The reasons for that are complex and his punishment was extreme.' Gregor sat back in his chair, his brows drawn down over his eyes as they studied Earl. If he'd thought the examination was over, he was wrong. The probing had been completed but Gregor was still weighing up the evidence. He could sense it, the mulling over the past, the assessment of the events Gregor had witnessed in Earl's mind and his own conflicted feelings. Yet even as the old warlock hesitated, Earl's conscience was clear, and he sensed that Gregor would judge well.

'So you have come to a decision?' Humphrey ventured.

'Yes.' Gregor let out a long breath.

Nea found a reserve of talent and poked a small hole in the magical cloak holding her down. Air rushed in and she breathed, gratefully, shallowly. As there was no reaction, she knew then that Drew hadn't noticed. She took a few more moments to garner her strength. To drain her, Drew would need to lift the cloak.

The pressure lifted. Drew came closer with wary footsteps. He wasn't assuming she was dead or unconscious yet. She held herself still, played dead.

Drew touched her and flipped her over. Her power hit him between the eyes. His head crashed against the bulkhead and he crumbled. She got to her feet and ran for the cabin. She needed to get the motor running. Needed to get back into hailing range. The anchor winched itself up as she took the chair.

As she turned the key to start the engine, a shadow fell on her. Turning, she saw that Drew stood in the doorway, one arm above his head grasping the upper part of the doorframe, blood leaking from behind his ear.

'You're cleverer than I expected. I like that. Not

the vacant moonface I first thought.' He gestured with his hand again and her face was held tight, fingers of power digging in, lifting her out of the chair and stretching her so that only the tips of her toes brushed the deck. He moved closer, bringing her face to his. 'I'm growing tired of this game. Just let me kill you.'

She brought up her knee and caught him in the groin, hard. They banged heads as he doubled over. Nea, released, was thrown against the cabin's built-in seating. Dazed, she shook her head and then used her talent to let out the throttle. Then she threw a potent force against the dark warlock. He lifted out through the doorway, arms flailing. As her power waned he caught the rail with his hand and halted his trip overboard. The boat lurched as it hit a swell and then turned in circles, the engine revving and no one at the wheel.

❦

Earl let go of the tension in his body, the clenching of his jaw he didn't know he'd been doing. The throb in his head came back with a vengeance.

'Stand up, Earl Pressonville, and hear the judgement of your examiners.' Hilda's voice was clear and it sent tingles over his skin. It was like a song, evocative and demanding.

On their feet and surrounding him, the three of them stepped back and he rose to his feet. The pain of the examination was distant now, fading fast, and he had to steady himself with a hand on the back of the chair. The pain was not physical or deliberately inflicted. The act of having others examine one's mind meant their talent intruded into your own. The pressure was what caused the hurt and left one weakened. His talent had been bled off so that theirs could delve inside his mind, remove his resistance and open him up, like cleaving a book in two.

As he stood there waiting to hear what they had to say, he was cleansed after revealing all of his misdeeds. He'd been young and stupid, and examining them now he realized that Humphrey was right. Pris has spelled him, subtly but effectively. He'd been lost the moment he'd stepped through her door and allowed himself to be exposed to her darkness. He was not totally innocent, as he had lacked the will to break free. He'd allowed his most base desires to take over. He blinked.

'Earl Pressonville, we find you not guilty of crimes against the folk. You may live among us, provided we have your oath that you will abstain from blood magic and from consorting with dark folk,' Gregor said.

'Thank you,' he whispered, not quite believing Gregor's words. 'Thank you,' he said in a louder voice. 'I will never use blood magic or knowingly consort with dark ones.'

All he could think was that he was free to be with Nea, to have a life with her. A smile lit his face at the same time that tears stung his eyes. He sent out his mind to touch Nea's to let her know but she wasn't there. Wasn't waiting.

He frowned. Where was she? He was about to widen his search and almost missed the next words from Gregor.

'I request that you move to another coven,' Gregor said, his voice hard.

'Another coven?' Earl swallowed, not quite understanding but feeling the dread anyway, as if the gravity of those words impacted before their meaning did.

'Sydney will take you in if I vouch for you.'

'But why?' Earl frowned and then looked between them.

'You are not welcome here.'

'But ... Nea?'

'You are not welcome to her either.'

'Gregor,' Hilda said, concern in her voice. 'You cannot do that. It's Nea's decision. He's not guilty.'

Gregor turned on her. 'She is my kin and I won't have her giving her life to him.'

'But she loves him, Gregor. You of all people should understand that. You who gave up so much for love.'

Gregor lowered his shoulders, unclenched his fists. 'I can't bear it.'

Hilda reached up and touched his cheek affectionately. 'If you want her in your life, you must. She will follow him, of that I'm sure. Would you send her away from you? From us?'

He shook his head. 'She won't choose him over me.'

'Oh Gregor. You would do that to her? Would you really? She loves you more than life.'

Gregor turned to face her, his lips drawn into a straight line. 'You should stop there, Hilda.'

'Or what? You'll make me choose too?'

He scoffed. 'You're being ridiculous. I'm not making you choose.'

'Yes, you are. You're making me choose between you and what is right.'

Gregor inhaled loudly, his head jerking back.

Hilda went on. 'I love you Gregor Royston, but I'll not stand by and watch you ruin Nea's future and the future of this man here. You're a stubborn old coot and I know you've got a powerful memory, but you have a strong sense of right too.'

Gregor turned away from her, his fists clenching.

'Look at this young man,' she said getting in his way. 'Look at him without prejudice,' she said pointing. Gregor did as she asked and he stood there, passive as the old man's powerful gaze bored into him. 'He's got talent and he's got love in him. Remember how you were and what you did for love when you were his age? You turned your back on everything you knew to be with Bess. Let him have that. Let Nea have that. Let them see where their love will take them.'

Gregor lifted his eyes to the ceiling. 'It's so hard to let go of the past. I remember his arrogance … his disregard for authority. The coven was young then; he nearly drove a wedge, nearly destroyed it all.'

'No, he didn't. You thought he did, but you saw through his memories that it wasn't the case. It was Pris. The dark witch you had a truce with. She was the destabilizing influence, the one who really threatened your power.'

Gregor nodded, his usually bright eyes shadowed, but he said nothing.

'Gregor?' Hilda reached out and touched his hand gently.

Turning to her, he touched Hilda's cheek affectionately, like a man surrendering. 'Teach me how … how to forgive … to forget …'

She smiled sadly. 'I can tell you are ready to do that. You don't need me to teach you. Now, let matters take their course. If Nea chooses him as her mate you will accept it. If they do not make a match of it then you will accept that too.'

The old warlock sniffed and rubbed his forehead. 'Okay. I will try.'

Hilda's eyebrow lifted, her dark gaze fixed on him.

A slight grin brightened his expression. 'I won't interfere. My word on that.'

Hilda smiled, her eyes sparkling with delight and affection. She reached down and took the old warlock's hand and squeezed. 'Your word is accepted.'

Then Gregor shifted so that he could look Earl straight in the eye. 'But you'll have no help from me either.'

CHAPTER THIRTEEN

rew! Danger rang out like a klaxon in her mind. Drew was going to climb aboard again. She had to get to the controls. Crawling along the bucking deck, she inched forward. Her talent was weakened and trying to steady the controls was like trying to pick up a dropped egg from the floor. It slid and avoided her touch.

With a sudden lurch, she glanced behind her. Drew was still holding on but his attempt to climb aboard had stalled. Yet she couldn't let the boat careen here and there. It would be dangerous. She managed to throttle back and the boat calmed. With a thud of her heart, she heard his step when he climbed back on board. She left the conn to meet him.

'Thought you'd get away from me, did you?' Drew asked as he stepped in front of her.

'I thought to make it difficult for you, yes.' Her voice came over sounding confident.

His eyes widened. She grinned fiercely, glad that he wasn't expecting that. He'd wanted a fearful response. It fed his ego, his sense of power. But she wasn't going to play that game anymore. All she cared about was under threat. Earl's life was on the line for saving her life. Drew was the one who should be on trial, the one who should be facing death as punishment for his crimes. The fact he wasn't annoyed her. What was happening to Earl right now? Would he pass through his judgement?

Drew flung power at her again and she cried out in pain. It hurt. Looking down, she saw her clothes were singed and her flesh red from the heat. Half bent over, she struggled to maintain her concentration. Distant thunder teased her ears. A storm was coming and she had a dark warlock on a boat with her and she didn't know what was happening with Earl. She wasn't going to make it after all. The magical burn travelled along her senses. She huddled there, panting.

'Bitch. You think you can outwit me?'

All he got back from her was a whimper.

His head jerked around suddenly. 'Take me into Swansea and I'll let you live.'

Her head rocked back at this change in tack. 'If you're so bloody powerful you don't need me. Take yourself.'

'I'm quite able but I need insurance.'

'Insurance? Me?' Nea laughed. 'Why? No one is even looking for you.'

The warlock sneered at her. 'Nice try, but they are searching. Getting close.' Thunder boomed as a sudden gust hit. 'I haven't finished with you yet ...'

Waves were peaking, stirred up by the storm. Thick drops of rain rattled the roof of the cabin and slicked the deck. She held on and panted through the pain. They were on a lake but it was open to the sea.

Suddenly, the boat bucked as if lifted by a hand and then dropped. Drew stumbled, his weight overbalanced. Holding on securely and expecting the boat's behavior in storm-tossed water, she focused her talent to tip him farther. Her feet were planted wide and she rode the boat's turbulent passage. She sent a thrum of power into the motor.

Unfortunately, Drew recovered his balance. He sent another burst of power at her, this time hitting her knee. She went down with a screech of pain. The motor eased back and the boat bobbed with the turbulence and insufficient thrust.

The next time the deck lurched, she fell forward and hit her forehead and bumped her nose. Pain radiated through her. This was it. *Oh Earl, I'm sorry.*

Satisfied that Gregor was giving him a chance, Earl was keen to tell Nea the news. She hadn't been close when he'd tried to sense where she was. Frowning, he sent his talent further and still he could not locate her.

'Where's Nea?' he asked Gregor and Hilda.

Gregor frowned and Earl detected his talent as it swept by him like a gentle wave. 'Not close by,' he said. He walked to the sliding door. 'The boat's gone. She's out on the lake.'

A sense of foreboding tingled his skin. 'I should be able to reach her.' He walked out the door, down through the garden to the shore. Hilda and Gregor's quiet chatter advised him they were following on behind.

He'd been able to touch Nea from afar. He knew the taste and feel of her from that moment she had touched him with her essence. The first sweep failed to locate her. 'Why did she leave?' he said.

Hilda shrugged, then slid her hand into Gregor's. 'She would have found it hard to be near your pain.'

Branches crashed together and leaves rattled in the wind. His gaze shot upwards. Dark cumulous clouds marched across the sky, eating up the last of the sun. The lake was turbulent and grey. There were no boats to be seen.

'She's out in that?'

Gregor nodded. 'She knows better than to go out in a storm. She'd take shelter, wait it out.' He ranged out with his power. 'I can't detect her.' He shook his head. 'Too weak? Blast it.'

Hilda sniffed the air. 'The storm is new. She's been gone a long time. Something's not right, though.'

Earl rocked back on his heels. 'Nea?' he cried out. There was a slight touch of her against his mind. Closing his eyes, he tried to capture that thread of her that had reached out to him. 'She's in trouble. It's Drew.'

'Where?' Gregor asked.

'On the other side of the lake. She's in pain, injured.'

'I'll contact some members of the coven. There are some on that side of the lake.'

'I'm going after her,' Earl said. He pulled off his sweater.

'You're going to swim?' Gregor asked. 'In that?'

The lake was a boiling grey mess. Earl stalled. 'Yes! No! I don't know. I can't lose her.'

Hilda glared at them both. 'You two. Earl is a conjurer. He is strong and determined.'

Gregor's head jerked back. 'You mean?'

'Yes. He can think himself there.'

'I can't. I have a body now. It's different.'

'It's no different,' Hilda said. 'You still have that other body of yours. Use this flesh one—' She pinched the skin of his arm. '—as your anchor.'

Nea's pain was now throbbing in his mind. If he didn't go to her, he could be too late and all that he had done to be with her would be for naught. He had to try.

Kneeling down, he closed his eyes and then drew out of himself, following the thread of her. He was a conjurer and he could manipulate light and some matter to create scenes. Without flesh, he could just think himself there.

The deck solidified under his feet. Drew hunched over Nea, who sprawled on the deck, her upper body supported by the bulkhead. They hadn't noticed him. Drew was getting ready to hurl power into her and it seemed at first glance that she was unconscious. Then all of a sudden, she reached out with her reader talent, but instead of being something porous that could sink into the other warlock, it came out solid.

At the same time, the boat revved and surged forward. Her power and the momentum of the boat coincided. Drew flew straight out at an angle. As Earl was in specter form he wasn't dislodged from his feet when the deck lurched beneath him. In a blink of an eye, Drew was gone.

Earl looked and there was no sign of Drew beneath a cauldron of gray waves. His eyes sought her.

'Nea?'

She turned towards him. 'Earl?' She squinted at him, at his conjured body. 'Are you dead again?' A sob burst out of her. 'No. Oh Goddess no!'

In an instant he was with her. 'No. I came to find you. I left my flesh behind. Hilda and Gregor are with me.'

She cried then, sobbing hard. 'Earl … I thought I'd lost you.'

'You're hurt,' he said as he trailed a ghostly hand along her burn.

She steadied herself, swallowing her tears. 'The judgement?'

'I'm not guilty.'

Her tear-stained gaze met his. 'I know that.' She shrugged. 'I'm glad they saw it too.'

Struggling to her feet, she half crawled to the steering wheel and then upped the power to the motor. She drove into some sheeting rain and it covered the bow with water. It lessened to sprinkling until another squall hit. It wasn't long before the shore came into sight.

'I will go back now.' Earl hoped he knew how to regain control of his body. It was hard to leave it, the warm living flesh.

She looked up at him. 'Thank you for coming for me.'

He nodded and then he was back on the shore. It was like being winded. Air was hard to draw into his lungs—it was like his diaphragm was rigid. Dark spots ripened in his vision and his fingers and toes tingled, pins and needles registering as pain.

He heard the motor of the boat as he face planted into the grass. Hilda's hands grabbed at him, turned his face so he could breathe. Gregor lumbered over. 'Is he all right?'

Hilda ran her hands over him. 'Yes, he's back.'

A low moan escaped him. That had hurt. He tried moving his hands but they were like thick gloves and his feet were numb stumps. 'I … I can't…' He stopped trying to talk.

'There, there, just breathe for now.' Hilda's voice was soothing and she ran her fingers through his hair.

'Nea … hurt,' was all he could get out.

Gregor jogged to the jetty. The motor coughed and slurred before the boat slowed and the momentum of the storm kept propelling it. The aftertaste of power let him know that Gregor was bringing Nea in safely with his talent.

Hilda sat him up and through hazy vision he noted Nea was slumped at the control. He tried to move, but was held down by Hilda. 'Let Gregor fetch her. I suspect you both will need some care and bed rest.'

Gregor leaped on board and tossed the ropes over, and they tied themselves as he went to Nea and lifted her gently in his arms. He was chanting over her, and she lifted her hand and touched her grandfather's ear before dropping it.

Hilda stood up. 'She'll be okay. I don't think it's serious.'

'Drew fell overboard,' Earl said, finding his tongue and mouth were in sync.

Hilda's eyes flashed. 'Dead?'

He shrugged. 'Not sure. Too hard to tell. I wasn't paying attention as there was too much going on. Nea fought him.' He was coming to terms with that. She'd held her own against a powerful dark warlock.

Hilda scrunched her lips. 'Pity. We could rest easier if he were … gone.'

'Hilda … Nea.' He frowned, trying to order his thoughts and beliefs. 'Nea did something extraordinary out there today. I know she's a reader, but she used her power in a different way. Like she polarized it, made it more like an enforcer's power.'

Hilda helped him to stand. 'Today she was tested and found her inner strength. Her talent was always wasted here, just looking after Gregor.' She peered up at him. 'You both have a lot of talent that could be put to good use for the coven, for the folk.'

'Then Nea and I have a lot to talk about.'

Hilda smiled. 'Isn't that wonderful?'

'Certainly is.' His smile matched hers.

With that, Hilda helped him into the house. As they entered, Siv arrived and immediately, Hilda started bossing him about. 'Come and help me with this one. No, wait—see to Nea. Quickly, man, she's been hurt.'

Siv wobbled his head, trying to work out which command to comply with when Gregor called out and he raced up the stairs.

❀

Nea came in. 'Is he all right?' she asked Hilda, who had almost overdosed him on any remedy she had on hand.

Earl was feeling more like himself, more aligned within his spirit body and his flesh. Not quite as he should be, but better. There was still the sensation like the floor was about to fall away from his feet and he would jerk to brace himself. Yet, it was less pronounced. He was more present and occupying his body. Repeating the out-of-body experience wasn't on his list of Things To Do in the near future.

Hilda took the cup, checked he'd drunk the contents, and nodded. 'Nothing that a bit of rest won't fix. You let him recover, won't you?'

Nea blushed. 'Of course. I don't know what you mean.'

She looked at him, her head cocked to the side as if to say 'defend me'.

'Nea and I want to be alone to recuperate,' Earl said and grinned.

Hilda chuckled. 'Recuperate? I've not heard it called that before.'

Nea's cheeks flamed but before she could launch into a denial, the older witch waved her hands dismissively and marched out of the room. The door smacked shut behind her.

Earl stood and they faced each other across the room, her room. In the look they shared, so much passed between them: affection, relief, love, desire.

Earl came forward and met her, brushing her blonde hair off her forehead and kissing the tip of her freckled nose. She was warm and whole and he could not believe his luck, this life, this moment. Her blue eyes held him and he opened to her so she could taste all that he felt and the clumsiness of words were avoided.

Her reader talent swept over him and he sucked in a breath. The brush of her talent was strong, with a confidence born of finding a core of strength. 'You love me,' she said simply.

Earl smiled. 'You love me.' It was there for him to read, to taste, to mingle with. A bright, shining light that was Nea's essence warmed him. No wonder she'd been able to rouse him and sweep his spirit clean.

Her grin grew into a full-toothed smile, her eyes twinkling with delight. 'I surely do. But are you going to stand around gaping at me or are we going to get serious about this?'

He chuckled softly, running his finger along her chin and then brushing a teasing kiss on her lips. 'What's the hurry? We have the rest of our lives to enjoy sex.'

Her smile dropped. Then before he could blink she'd tipped him onto the bed and positioned herself on top of him. 'You are not even close to being funny. I happen to know that you're as keen as I am to get busy.'

He laughed again. 'I can't hide anything from you.'

Her grin was back and she peeled off her T-shirt.

She wasn't wearing a bra. He sat up to grab a nipple in his mouth. When he latched on she let out a gasp. The silken feel of her skin under his fingertips and the way he moved up the contours of her back caused his senses to overload in the most wonderful way. How had he ever lived without a whole body, without touch and smell and taste?

After enjoying himself in this position for ten minutes or so and listening to the joyous gasps of delight coming from Nea, he flipped her over. She let out a yelp and then giggled when he licked a pathway between her breasts to her neck where he suckled some more, making her groan in delight. Her arousal spilled out of every pore of her and he supped on it like life itself.

Lifting himself free for a moment, he shucked his T-shirt and peeled off his jeans. Nea wiggled on the bed, freeing herself of the last of her clothes, and lay naked before him, more heat in her eyes than in the setting sun. Yet, he wasn't afraid of her intensity. It pleased him because his own love and desire matched hers.

Their bodies met. Heat on heat. Muscle on muscle. Moist on moist. Earl was transported into realm of sensory richness. Touches of lips, of fingers, of skin on skin, of erection welcomed into her moist folds. Her muscles clenched him tight, increasing the friction of each thrust. The joyous sound of her responses, her glorious abandonment to their lovemaking—how could he ever have desired anything else?

He'd not known how linked one could be, mind, body and spirit. Not until Nea had shone her light on him.

His new body was adjusting to life. He fitted perfectly to her form, catching her cry as he slid inside her again and again, joining to the rhythm. The temptation to lose himself in the moment almost overcame him. His body's response to making love threatened to spill out of him.

Her eager kisses drew him into her instead. Her whispers settled him down into his body, into her, and then the blissful moment came and he thought he'd be lost forever.

When his heart slowed and his breathing was normal again, he roused with his limbs entwined with Nea's, her arms encircling him, and he knew the rightness of his being. This was where he was going to stay. He bent his head down and kissed the top of her head and she sighed sleepily.

Riley, Nea's father, stood beside her, passing the care of her to Earl Pressonville. Gregor Royston, head of the Lake Macquarie coven, officiated at their mating ceremony.

Nea was beyond joy. Dressed in a stunning blue gown, she glowed with confidence and love. Her blonde hair was straight down her back and her makeup was minimal. Her natural beauty was enough for Earl and for her too. If she had asked herself six months ago where she would be now, it would not have been here, not being mated to Earl, an amazing warlock, with her family surrounding her. It had been a hard and unusual road, but it had been worth it.

Earl gazed into eyes as she spoke her promises. At the same time, he detailed how he wanted to make love to her, whispering the words into her mind. Her body was alive to arousal. That he could do that with words and a look was no surprise. He was an extraordinary warlock. They had formed a plan that they would train to be battle mages and defend their people from the dark ones threatening folk and humans alike. Both of them had grown in talent and with hard work, more strength and skill would come.

Gregor had offered them the flat downstairs as a home and they'd agreed to it. Hilda had taken over the 'looking after' of Gregor and that suited Nea. It suited Gregor too, by the looks of things. She had her own man to look after now. Actually, it was the other way around. He looked after her.

Gregor had gotten over all of his mistrust of Earl eventually. Hilda had helped him realize that by reminding him that Nea wasn't going to go away to Sydney or overseas, and that at the rate she and Earl copulated, they'd likely have six children in the next five years. Hilda's arithmetic was a bit off. At least, Nea hoped it was.

Her gaze passed over the people who were the closest to her, noting the love and happiness as they shared a major life celebration. Hilda winked at her and Nea laughed. Hilda was so good for them all.

Then her gaze locked with Earl's and she repeated her vows directly into his mind, feeling the right of them. He was a man who knew what was important in life. Nea was important to his life and she had to admit that he was just as necessary to her.

The End

ACKNOWLEDGEMENTS 2016

I have to acknowledge the wonderful critique of Kate Cuthbert in getting this story in shape and fit for publication. It has been a very difficult story for me to write, so hard I nearly gave up on it. That would have been my first abandoned story ever!

I'd also like to thank Harlequin Escape for their support in publishing the *Spellbound in Sydney* series. To my good buddy Nicole goes thanks for beta reading, making suggestions and just being there to cheer me on. Thank you also to readers who have read *Spiritbound* and *Bespelled*. I hope you enjoy *Invoked*. It's such a good feeling knowing that people have read and liked your work so feel free to contact me online.

Dani

ACKNOWLEDGEMENTS 2020

The rights of this book returned to me in 2019 and so in 2020 I am rereleasing it. The story is essentially the same but I have made a few modifications. As I mentioned in 2016, this story was hard to write for me. It was a challenge and I hope you enjoy the results of my efforts.

There might be more stories in this world in future. I have a few ideas.

Happy reading.

Dani

ABOUT THE AUTHOR

Dani Kristoff is an Australian author based in Canberra, the nation's capital. She delights in reading and writing paranormal romance. For the close to twenty years, she been concentrating her efforts on science fiction, fantasy and horror. In 2016, she left the public service to pursue a PhD at the University of Canberra. Her research area is feminism in popular romance fiction, which means she gets to read retro Mills & Boon, which is no hardship at all. Her partner, Matthew, is also a writer and they live in a big house overlooking the mountains.

Dani has two paranormal series going, the first being *The Spellbound Series*, which features witches and is mostly set in Sydney. She also has a darker, more erotic series set in a different world system, starting with *The Sorcerer's Spell*, to be followed up with *The Changeling Curse*. *The Sorcerer's Spell* is based in Canberra and features sorcerers and werewolves and other magical creatures. It has a particularly nasty sorceress for a villain who uses sex to fuel her magic.

9 781922 360045